Love Woven in Time

A Ligonier Golden Romance

Karen Malena

Lamb Books

ISBN-13:978-0692367148 (Lamb Books)
ISBN-10: 0692367144
Copyright 2015 Karen Malena

Contact the author on Facebook at:

https://www.facebook.com/Karen-Malena-author

Visit Karen's blog filled with inspirational stories at, *The Finch's Nest* at http://karenmalena.blogspot.com/

Photograph on the cover of the Ligonier Diamond taken by Heather Roddy. Thank you.

DEDICATION

For my parents, Rich and Eileen

and the true love they've shared

for over fifty years

THIS BOOK BELONGS TO

CONTENTS

ACKNOWLEDGMENTS

First of all I'd like to thank you, the reader for choosing this book.

I'd also like to thank my husband Jim and son, Matt for their encouragement and being my biggest cheerleaders.

A very special thank you to Bette Fisher and author Alicia Stankay for working so diligently with me on editing and Lamb Books for taking on another project with me.

This book wouldn't have been possible without the great input of Carol Howell, Dementia specialist and author of Let's Talk Dementia: A Caregiver's Guide. I'd like to thank her for the times I sent her snippets to read and received great suggestions on making the story better. The facts about dementia and Alzheimer's are used with careful consideration from her and the vitamin deficiency is a true health issue.

To Michelle Gardner of Thisteldown at Seger House and Bo Peeps Fine Yarns, I owe a huge debt of thanks as well. I appreciate her cheerful ways and help with the beautiful town of Ligonier. Also I must mention Jason at Equine Chic, Second Chapter Books and Debi Stoll of Scamp's Toffee of Ligonier for allowing me to use your charming shops as the backdrop to the town I love so much. Kathy Balentine, Teri Hirko, Sheryl Arbogast, Bob Leonard, Dan Morris and the others from the wonderful Facebook page *Ligonier and the People Who Love it There* for all the information and photographs they provided me with.

A major thank you to Heather Roddy for the stunning photograph on the cover of the Ligonier gazebo.

I'd like to thank my brother Rick Mattia for the information on autism and Asperger's. The knowledge he shared is very close to his heart as he has worked closely with children who have these disorders for many years.

Having said all that, although I use some real Pennsylvania towns in this book, I do take liberties with them at times. I encourage you to visit the real town of Ligonier, Pennsylvania and hope you find it as alluring as me and my husband.

Finally, I'd like to thank my Heavenly Father who plants and waters the seeds of inspiration.

Chapter One

Rose Warner counted the loops of her crocheting, slipping the last stitch over the hook, wincing as pain shot through her swollen fingers. The needle clinked to the floor, and as she bent to retrieve it, arthritis with more tendrils of pain stabbed pointy fingers into her lower back.

Not what I used to be, she sighed. *Darn, tired body.* Yet at seventy- two, Rose counted herself lucky. Unlike many of the older people in this place she had no major health issues, a full head of wavy salt and pepper hair, and the ability to walk on her own.

She resided in Huntington Home for Seniors on the ground floor of a community for elderly folks who still lived on their own with minor assistance. Nestled in the mountains of Chestnut Ridge in Ligonier, Pennsylvania, the care facility sat upon acres of lush farmland. Each individual apartment connected to one another, with a huge activity room at the center of the complex and a medical building behind it.

Her daughter, Toni, recently persuaded Rose to live out her remaining years here, telling her it would be good for her to be around others her age. "There are so many activities for you to do, Mama," Toni had said, as she waved goodbye in her Mercedes.

That was almost four months ago. Rose hadn't seen her daughter since. Sometimes when she heard the sound of a car in front of her building, and the toot of a horn, she imagined Toni stopping by for a visit. Seconds would pass, turning into minutes, which turned into an hour, and Rose knew her daughter wasn't really there.

The vinyl baby doll, the secret Rose hid most of her life, lay swaddled upon her lap in one of the small afghans she'd crocheted in her younger years. Rose laid the soft, wooly yarn onto the end table next to her, cradling the tiny doll in her arms. She crooned a sweet lullaby and then pulled herself up from her grandma's rocking chair, laying her baby upon the cushions of her velveteen couch.

Alex had known. . .

Rose sighed as she thought of her good husband Alex. Their marriage lasted forty-five years until Alex's heart had given out one day while he tended their cherished flower garden. Alex had been her rock with his quiet strength.

"At least I have you, Buttons," she said to the calico cat blinking lazily up at her. "Come on, time for you to eat." Rose walked ahead of the pet she'd owned for many years into the small kitchen.

The care facility that housed her was small, clean and comfortable. It hadn't been easy adjusting at first, leaving behind a beautiful house, but walking the stairs several times daily wasn't something she missed. With the paintings she'd acquired through the years gracing her walls, the few Hummel statues she'd collected, and the blankets she'd crocheted with such care, it felt like home now.

As Rose was about to place a spoonful of tuna cat food onto a plate for Buttons, she heard the sound of car doors slamming outside her kitchen window. Parting the thin floral curtains a bit, she watched as two men began pulling furniture from a small rental moving van. A second vehicle pulled into another space, and a young, pretty redhead, around her daughter's age, helped an elderly man out of the passenger side.

The man was clearly upset, wiping his swollen, red eyes on the sleeve of his sweater. Rose could see the young lady appeared to speak gently to him, ushering him toward an apartment a few doors down from her. Rose watched a moment longer, craning her neck to view the four of them, until they disappeared through the door of apartment 5-C.

Rose headed back into her small living room, turning on the television to the classic movie channel. An old favorite of hers, *To Kill a Mockingbird*, was about half over. Rose settled in with her crocheting once again, the rhythmic rocking of the chair lulling her. Atticus Finch defended Tom Robinson on the screen before her.

Rose's mind wandered and sleep overtook her, the yarn and crochet hook dropping onto her lap. In the dream, she held the child she'd lost, the perfect baby boy, her miracle. One more time, she rocked him gently in her dream as he suckled at her breast.

Rose awoke with a start, a pang of longing so fierce it stole the breath from her for a moment. She remembered where she was, and let the thoughts of the little baby she'd named Nathaniel drift away. Reaching over to the swaddled doll, caressing it lightly, she turned the television off.

The sun slanted through the living room windows, dust motes dancing upon the air. Buttons curled around her feet, letting out a sleepy yawn.

The last remnants of the dream began to fade, leaving Rose empty. "I won't do this," she said aloud. Though sadness choked her, Rose picked up her favorite sweater and headed out the door to the small porch area of her apartment.

A slight breeze swayed the branches of the Japanese maple in her yard, the last rays of sun on the early summer day turning the world a golden hue.

The family she'd watched earlier in the day appeared to be bringing the last of the belongings into 5-C. The young woman waved at Rose as she started walking toward her.

"Hello," she said, extending a delicate hand. "I'm Abby. Abby Carson. Nice to meet you." Her genuine smile lit up a pretty face. Her auburn hair, flecked with gold, sparkled in the dwindling light of day. Small freckles dotted her cream-colored cheeks.

"Well, it's nice to meet you too, honey. I'm Rose Warner." Rose pulled her sweater a bit more tightly around her. "Nice night."

"Yes, I guess it is," Abby said, glancing back over her shoulder, then quickly back at Rose.

"May I ask you a favor, Rose?" The lovely smile disappeared and concern etched itself on Abby's face.

"If it's in my power," Rose said. "Go ahead, ask."

"My brothers and I are finishing up getting Dad settled in a few doors down. This hasn't been one of my family's best days." Abby looked down, fidgeting with the buttons on her crisp, cotton blouse. "Would you be able to look out for Dad from time to time? I know it's a lot, but if he could get to know someone here, perhaps he wouldn't feel so lost."

"Well, I'm not the best welcoming committee," Rose said, "but I'll be glad to talk to him sometime. Yes, you can count on it."

Abby smiled again, and lowered her voice a bit.

"I tried telling them Dad could stay in his house. I really

fought for him, you know?" Abby pleaded with her clear hazel eyes, as if willing Rose to say something to absolve her. "His mind's going a bit, and he started falling. I'd love to take him in with me, but I have three small children and too many flights of stairs."

Rose put a hand on Abby's arm. "Listen, if it makes you feel better, I think you did the right thing. I'm sure your father will be fine here. They check on us several times a day. We have meals in the common room and transportation to all doctor visits. In some ways, this is better than living in our big, quiet homes. As I see it, you did your dad a favor."

"I hope you're right," Abby said as one of her brother's motioned for her. "I have to go. It was nice talking with you, Rose. I'll be by at least twice a week to check on Dad. I hope to see you again." Abby kissed Rose on the cheek and then turned to leave. "Thanks for listening."

Rose stood a few moments and watched Abby and one of her brothers drive off in the car, while the other, the younger-looking one, screamed unintelligible words back into the apartment, his red face contorted with rage. The door slammed shut, leaving him standing alone on the front stoop. He braced his arms against the sides of the front door, his head hung low. He stood a moment longer, kicking the bottom of the door, and after glancing around, left in the van.

Rose put a hand to the cheek Abby had kissed, liking the

quick show of emotion. The girl seemed genuinely concerned for her father. The strange scene with the son, however. . . Rose's mind changed gears and she thought about the man sitting there alone, his first night in a new place.

Chapter Two

*R*ose awoke early the next morning. After a cup of coffee and a few salmon treats for Buttons, she set out to bake an apple pie for her new neighbor. *Nothing like a good pie to cheer someone.*

Carefully rolling out the crust, paring tart Granny Smith apples, sprinkling cinnamon and sugar, and dotting the dabs of butter, Rose popped it into the oven and set the timer. The aroma of baking apples lay in the air while Rose washed bowls, spoons and measuring cups in the soapy water of the kitchen sink.

At ten a.m., Rose bundled the still warm pie, and a deep, maroon-colored lap afghan into a large paper shopping bag to bring to the gentleman in 5-C.

I hope he doesn't think I'm crazy, she thought while she tapped at his door, fumbling for the right words to say.

After several raps, the door opened a crack, and the bluest eyes she'd ever seen peered out at Rose. She held up the bag of goodies. "Good morning," she said. "I'm the welcoming committee."

The man took a step back, opening the door for her to enter his living room. "I didn't know anyone would be welcoming me," he said.

Rose chuckled. "No, I'm just a neighbor. I came by to say hello and bring you a few things." She walked into the room, taking in the simple, yet homey furnishings, and handed him the bag.

"Oh, I'm sorry," Rose said. "I'm Rose Warner."

The man smiled at her, and the blue eyes twinkled in a still handsome face. Though he was bent slightly from age, he carried himself with an air of dignity. *Retired army colonel*, Rose thought.

"Harry McMillen at your service," the man said, laying the bag onto a coffee table and taking Rose's hand in his own. "A pleasure to meet you."

"I hope you like what I brought you," she said. "I know what it can feel like not knowing anyone in a strange, new place." She turned to go. "I don't want to take up your time."

"No, please stay. I'd love to have someone to talk with." Harry picked up the bag and motioned for her to follow him into his kitchen. "Please sit." He pulled a chair out for her, and then proceeded to remove items from the bag. He laid the warm pie, wrapped in several layers of foil, onto the kitchen table. As he pulled the blanket from the bottom, a tear trickled from the corner of one eye, and he swiped at it with his hand.

"I'm sorry," he said. "Getting old and sentimental, I guess. This is very kind of you, uh, forgive me. Your name slipped my mind already."

"Trust me, I understand the sentimental part. I'm the queen of it, actually," she laughed, "and the name is Rose, like a flower."

"How about some coffee, Rose?" Harry asked, changing the subject, his face turning crimson. "Or do you prefer tea? We must have a piece of whatever it is you've baked." He shuffled to a cupboard.

"Oh, I've had my quota of coffee for the day. I'll join you in a slice of the apple pie though."

As Harry began laying plates on the kitchen table, Rose noticed a huge, leather-bound book in the center. It lay open and had several well-worn bookmarks sticking out of it.

"You a reader?" she asked.

"Not much of one," Harry answered. "Just my Bible."

Rose winced as if someone had hit her. A Bible. Conviction, guilt and despair. No, she never had much to do with one. She changed the subject.

"How was your first night? I have to admit, I peeked yesterday when you and your family arrived. I couldn't help but notice, you seemed a bit upset." She cut into the slice of pie before her, while Harry finished pouring coffee for himself. He sat near her at the table, and bowed his head for a moment, then began digging into his own piece.

"It wasn't an easy day," he said, through a mouthful of pie. "I thought I'd pass on to the great beyond in the home I'd shared with my wife in Latrobe, but my kids had other plans."

"Oh, I know all about that," Rose said. "It was my daughter's idea for me to live here. I wasn't crazy about it at first, but I'm actually starting to enjoy the activities and outings. It's nice seeing people every day. It was getting a bit lonely in my house." Rose finished the pie and wiped her mouth with a floral paper napkin Harry had set near her.

"I just wish my daughter would drop by though." Rose shook her head. "What about you, Harry?"

"Well, I think I'll be alright," he said. "My children were worried mostly about the flights of stairs in my house. I took a pretty bad fall last year and fractured a few ribs." He winced at the thought, patting his right side and indicating where he'd hurt himself. "I never wanted to be a burden to my family, so I agreed to this move." Harry sat back in the chair, and pushed his empty plate away. "The pie was wonderful, Rose."

Rose found herself liking Harry very much. He talked freely about his feelings, confiding in her like an old friend. He'd been sad leaving his home, but now he appeared eager for the next journey of his life. Harry talked about his faith, and made it seem like something almost alive and wonderful.

Rose felt caught up for a brief moment wishing she'd had something like that in her life.

There was no indication of the angry words passed between him and his son and Rose knew better than to pry.

"Well, I'm going to go," she said, glancing at the clock on his wall. "It's almost lunchtime and the van will be here soon to head to the common room." She walked toward the living room and then turned back to him. "You headed out to lunch today?"

"I hadn't planned on it, but if you're going, then I'd like that. Hold the van up for me if you would." At the front door, Harry reached out to stop her. "I can't thank you enough for your company this morning, Rose. What a blessing you've been." He patted her arm.

"See you in a bit," she said.

Later that day, long after the lunch dishes had been cleared, Rose and Harry strolled through the grounds of Huntington. Rose bent to retrieve a handful of violets in front of the medical building.

"I'm glad we decided to walk back," Rose said. "It's a wonderful day. I don't think they'll miss these, do you?" she asked Harry, placing the bouquet of flowers under her nose and breathing deep of the delicate fragrance.

"They sure are pretty," he said, "but not nearly as lovely as you, Rose."

"Harry, you're killing me," Rose laughed. "I haven't heard a pick-up line like that one in forever."

"Well, I'm not entirely sure it was a pick up line," he said. "You are pretty, Rose, inside and out. Just meeting you today and seeing your kindness has shown me goodness in another human being. I wish we'd have met earlier."

They strolled along in silence for a few moments, enjoying the warm afternoon sunshine, the sound of birds singing sweetly, and the company of one another.

"Well, here we are," Harry said as they neared the front of his building. "Would you care to come in for another piece of your wonderful pie?"

"My goodness, I can't eat another bite. But if you'd like, come over and sit with me on my little porch. I'd love to chat a bit longer."

After a few moments, they were seated facing one another. Rose lifted her face to the sunshine, enjoying the feel of it on her skin.

"Rose, tell me a little more about you. I've done most of the talking today. What's up with your daughter if you don't mind me asking? Do you have any idea why she doesn't stop by?"

Rose's face clouded over. She shut her eyes and swallowed. *Mustn't show him, mustn't let on. I know why my daughter hates me. I know.*

Instead, Rose changed the subject. "*You* have a lovely daughter, Harry. I met her yesterday when they moved you in. What a sweet girl. She seems to care very much about you."

"It wasn't always that way," he said. "As a matter of fact, my sons aren't exactly on the best of terms with me." He shook his head. "I'm afraid I wasn't a very good father."

Rose gasped. The handsome, gentle man before her, not a good father? How could it be? Harry carried himself with the air of old-fashioned manners, kindness and goodness. He had a Bible open for goodness sakes on his table. If that didn't show his character...

Harry appeared deep in thought. Several cars passed, and the sun hid behind a cloud. As a chill wind picked up, Rose drew her light sweater more tightly around her.

Harry looked directly at Rose. He pulled out a silk handkerchief and rubbed his eyes.

"It may not seem so now, but it's taken me years to truly give my life over to God, and make the necessary changes to be a better person. I've hurt my children terribly. In some ways, I don't blame them for not wanting me in their homes." He blew his nose loudly into the handkerchief.

Rose's mind wandered. Harry seemed to believe in what he spoke about, a loving God, forgiveness and change. If only it was that easy. Nothing could absolve Rose of her heavy burden, her horrible sin.

"If you'll excuse me, Harry, I need to take my afternoon pills. Perhaps we can chat another time." Rose got up, fumbling her key from a pocket in her sweater.

"Have I said something to offend you?" Harry asked.

"No, of course not. I'll talk with you again." She let herself into her apartment, leaving a stunned-looking Harry on her front stoop.

Rose shut the door, her back against it, breathing heavily. Images assaulted her: Mama's face contorted and screaming. Father sitting there shaking his head.

I was seventeen years old, only seventeen. Please, I don't want to live with this any longer.

Buttons weaved in and out of Rose's ankles, purring. Rose looked down. She hadn't meant to be so abrupt with her new friend Harry. But thinking about religion and all the implications of guilt, no, she wouldn't go there. She shook herself free of the painful memories. "Come on fellow, let's get you some lunch."

After she'd fed the cat and took her afternoon pills, Rose settled in with her crocheting. Her crusty but beloved Aunt Hilda had taught her when she was a young girl. Rose had always enjoyed the calmness crocheting brought her. Her fingers, though tender, flew over the yarn quickly slipping stitch after stitch from the hook. Several spools of soft yarn spilled from her craft bag, with Buttons batting one paw at the long strand she worked with.

Rose rocked back and forth in the chair, her eyes stealing every so often to the swaddled doll on the couch. She wanted to reach out and touch it, but a feeling of embarrassment crept over her. *I'm way too old for this.* Yet she'd heard some people began collecting stuffed animals as they aged. Rose felt her eyes closing, as an afternoon nap snuck up on her.

Rose Whitaker, seventeen years old, clutched her stomach as the violent pains coursed through her once again. Never before had she vomited like this. Perhaps the flu was going around. She wiped her mouth with the back of her hand, practically hanging over the commode in the family's bathroom. She flushed, watching the water swirl down the drain, straightened herself up, and headed to the sink. She splashed cold water onto a face that looked too pale in the mirror before her. Dark circles rimmed her eyes, and splotches of red dotted her cheeks.

As she left the room, her younger brother Billy bumped into her in the hallway. "Hey, Skip's on the porch talking to Mother."

Rose rolled her eyes. Talking to Mother! Skip Parkinson, a young man she'd been head over heels for the past six months wasn't someone her mother approved of. He was new in town, an older boy, and came from a family of common folks.

They'd met one day at the Penn Theater in downtown Pittsburgh. Rose and a few girlfriends had gone to see one of the Elvis Presley movies, and Skip had been standing outside against a battered old truck, skin-

tight jeans and leather jacket when the girls had come out of the show. He'd caught Rose's eye immediately and asked if she knew of any good places to eat lunch. Rose, ever the bold one had answered him, and the girls ended up at a small café down the block in the presence of the cocky, but very humorous, Skip.

Rose's friends sat horrified as Skip flattered Rose, sitting much too close to her and even putting his arm around her in the booth. He'd asked Rose if he could call her sometime and she'd shocked her friends by giving her phone number without hesitation.

The two had been inseparable ever since. Rose and Skip shared their hopes, dreams and deepest secrets, and their affection grew stronger as time passed. Skip had a tender side, and though life had thrown him some hard times, and he'd had his share of bitterness, Rose brought out everything that was good in him. He'd called her his angel and salvation. Rose fell in love with Skip, his brooding, but gentle ways only more endearing to her.

Rose's family didn't share her enthusiasm and Mother looked down her nose at him. Her family was well-to-do and Rose's Papa was one of the fortunate ones. He was boss at a local steel mill, a self-made man who came from poverty, but climbed the ranks with hard work and determination. They lived in Sewickley, Pennsylvania, a wealthy section of the Pittsburgh area. In the 1950's, their family wanted for nothing, though others around them lived in less than favorable conditions.

Shaking off her memories, Rose took a deep breath and walked out onto the porch. Willow trees swayed in the light breeze, the scent of honeysuckle lay in the air. Skip sat on the edge of the wicker chair, while

Mother sat stiffly upon the cushions of her small settee. Rose's heart leapt in her chest at the sight of her beau. Six feet tall, hard-muscled, with a head of coal black wavy hair, Skip was the epitome of bad boy and angel. Was it any wonder he'd stolen her heart so completely? Rose thought of little else throughout the day. She'd daydream about running away with him, fleeing from the watchful eyes of her mother.

"Hey, baby doll," Skip said, getting up and offering his seat to Rose. She sat, feeling her face turn crimson as her mother's eyes bored into her very soul.

"How's about you and me taking a little drive? Told your mom here we shouldn't be too long." And he winked lewdly at Rose. A feeling of heat stole through her and it wasn't only her face this time. She knew very well what Skip meant. A drive to him meant parking in some "lover's lane" and who knew what might happen then.

But as she was about to open her mouth to speak, a fierce wave of nausea overtook her. She ran to the edge of the porch, vomiting into the hydrangea bush. When she turned around, the look on her mother's face was horrible. Eyes bulging, veins popping out against the pearl necklace at her throat, her mother rose.

"Clean up that mess, young lady, and do it quickly. That's my prized flower, and I'll not have you soiling it." Turning to Skip, she pointed a finger at him. "And you, young man, I'll not have you stopping over at all hours of the day and night. You're not welcome to do so." She went into the house, slamming the door behind her.

Young Rose sank onto the settee, her face in her hands, sobs breaking free. Skip sat next to her and put an arm around her shoulders." Here, I have a handkerchief. Blow your nose like a good girl. I'll help you clean up, then maybe we can get on the road, huh?" He glanced nervously at the house.

"Why does she hate me so?" Rose sobbed louder. "I can't do anything right in her eyes. It's not like I meant for that to happen, not like I did it on purpose." She took the handkerchief, blowing her nose and dabbing at her eyes. "I hate her, Skip. She's a witch and I just despise her."

Rose stood, ignoring the swirling of her innards, grabbed Skip's hand, and pulled him from the porch toward his pickup truck. Spots danced before her eyes, and the world spun crazily. She never made it.

The next thing she remembered was lying in a hospital room, a nurse's face blurring before her, and her mother and father standing at the foot of the bed. Her father's beloved face showed concern, but Mother stood there, a menacing presence. She had a look Rose couldn't quite understand.

"Nurse, would you please leave the room?" her mother commanded. "We need to speak to our daughter."

When the nurse left, her mother wasted no time. She walked up to Rose and grabbed her arm, her well-manicured fingernails digging in. "What were you thinking, you slut? Oh yes, young lady, I know all about it. Sleeping around with that ugly young man. I had such plans for you, such dreams. You're about to throw it all away on having his child now?"

Rose gasped. Her father's face appeared older, tired. He clutched his *fedora in his hands, unable to meet her eyes.*

"What are you talking about, Mother?" Rose barely could speak above a whisper. An intravenous solution snaked into her other arm. What was her mother saying?

"When you fainted at the house, we rushed you to the hospital. They took some blood tests on you, and found out you're pregnant." Her mother spit the word out like poison.

Pregnant. A baby. Skip's baby. Rose glowed, happiness overtaking her mother's solemn mood. She loved Skip, and she'd be a good mama. She'd be able to leave her domineering mother behind and start a new life.

"Proper young ladies just do not do this," Mother said to her. "You'll get rid of this child immediately. I don't want my Women's Social Club to find out such a filthy, disgusting thing about you. And, you will never see that young man again, do you understand?"

Tears began to flow from Rose's eyes. She looked to her father for words of comfort, words he wasn't willing or able to give. Rose found her own voice finally.

"No, Mother, I will keep this baby and nobody will try to stop me. I love Skip. He and I will be fine. I want this baby more than anything." Sobs racked her body. Her father stepped toward her.

"Rosie," he said in a voice almost too quiet to hear, "I know how you think you feel right now. You must listen to Mother, though. You are much too young to be a mama. You are starting classes at the university next fall. Please think rationally, honey. There will be other children in your future, children with a good man and marriage."

Rose shook with anger. Sitting up, she pointed to the door. "Leave now, both of you! I don't want to see your faces ever again. I want to see Skip!"

"It's too late," her mother hissed. "I warned him to never step foot on our property again. And I found a facility that will remove that "thing" from you by the end of this week. I don't want to hear another word about it. Come on, William." Her parents left the room.

Rose lay there, unable to take a proper breath. They would take her baby from her without her consent. Could they do that? She shivered thinking of some "back alley" witchdoctor her mother had found.

For the next several hours, Rose caressed her stomach, speaking words of love to the child she'd never know. In her mind, she envisioned a boy, and she even named him. This baby was a miracle, not the demon spawn her mother thought it was. She longed to hold this child, nurse this child, but she'd never know him.

~*~

Rose got up from her nap, the memories all too clear. She grabbed her dolly, clutching it to her chest as sobs racked her body. Over and over she spoke, crooning, loving words to her baby, the one she never had. "I'm so sorry, Nathaniel, Mama's so sorry. I should have been stronger. I should have run away. Oh please, forgive me little one."

Buttons watched her from across the room, preening his whiskers, ears flattened at the sound of her crying. He walked over to Rose, sniffing at her. She bent down, patting his head, the tears beginning to subside.

I need my daughter. Oh Toni, I miss you so much. Taking a deep breath, Rose stood and walked to the portable phone lying atop the small oak desk in the corner of her living room. Quickly she dialed a number.

"Hey," the voice on the other end said, in a tinkling, sing-song way. "You've reached Toni's voice mail and you know what that means. Leave a message, please." Beep. Rose stared at the phone in her hand, uncertainty roiling within her. *Do I speak? What do I say?* She replaced the phone in its cradle. No, not now. Wait a bit longer. Toni would call her soon, wouldn't she?

Rose felt overcome by the memories. Reliving the worst time of her life blanketed her in sadness. She thought of Harry, her new friend. Yes, maybe a little time with him would help ease the pain. Picking up her sweater, she headed out the door to his apartment. When she rapped on his door and he didn't answer right away, she thought about changing her mind and heading back home. Then the door opened, and Harry's smiling face appeared.

"Rose, what a pleasant surprise. Come on in. Is everything okay?"

"I'm sorry to bother you again," she said, fidgeting with the buttons of her sweater, unable to meet his eyes.

"What is it, Rose?" Harry asked. He put a hand on her

shoulder.

"I'm an old fool, a stupid woman who's made so many mistakes," Rose said.

Harry took her hand and led Rose into his apartment.

"You asked about my daughter earlier, Harry. My daughter hates me. At least your children still speak with you. At least you've somehow made amends with them. I'm not sure what to do. . ." Her voice trailed off.

Harry walked Rose over to the sofa. "Wait here," he said. "I'll make some tea."

While Rose sat, her eyes fell upon the family photos which were lined up on a shelf above the television. Smiling pictures of a very nice-looking family, with Harry and what appeared to be his wife, at the center. There were no photos of this nature in Rose's world. Her daughter would never stay still long enough for a family portrait, and if she would have, there certainly wouldn't have been cheerful smiles on their faces.

She observed pictures on another wall, several pictures of Jesus, one with small children sitting at his feet. Each child looked up with wonder into the face before them, each of them with rapturous smiles. If only. . . Rose shivered.

Harry shuffled back into the room, placing a mug of aromatic tea before Rose. Under his other arm, the Bible stuck out, it's leather cover worn and a bit worse for wear.

He sat next to Rose, pulled a pair of reading glasses from

a shirt pocket and then opened the book, his fingers flipping through pages. He found a passage and read Psalm Forty out loud to her. Rose sipped tea, taking in the meaning of the words.

"So you see, Rose, we've all fallen short. We all sin, even David who wrote most of these Psalms. God still loves us unconditionally. There's nothing that can separate us from this."

Rose laid the cup of tea upon the coffee table and crossed her arms in front of her. Sitting back upon the couch, she closed her eyes and sighed. When she opened them again, she began to speak.

"I'd like to tell you a little about my daughter, if that's alright." When Harry nodded, Rose began. "Her name is Toni. It's short for Antoinette. She was the apple of my eye when she was born, a beautiful little girl, almost too lovely for words. Everyone doted on her, and that included me and her father. There wasn't much we held back, the answer 'no' wasn't in our vocabulary." Rose looked straight at Harry who sat attentive near her. He'd closed the Bible though it was still clasped in his hands.

"I. . ., I'd lost a baby when I was much younger. So there wasn't anything I wouldn't do for Toni. She was such a joy. But as she grew into a teenager, she became rebellious and spiteful. She accused me of ruining her life. And though I didn't understand it at the time, she bad-mouthed me any chance she could, especially with her Grandma Ruth, my mother. The two of them had grown very close, you see." Rose picked her tea up and held onto the mug.

"My mother and I hadn't been on good terms since I was in my late teens. She tried coming around again when Toni was born. As my daughter grew older, Mama really began spoiling her. I think Toni was everything I wasn't. Little by little, we lost our daughter. When she left for college, we barely saw her. When she returned one time, she told me she hated me and everything I stood for. It's been strained ever since." Rose stopped to catch her breath, taking a sip of tea.

"I'm so sorry, Rose," Harry said, slipping his arm through hers. "It must hurt you terribly. What is it with people sometimes?" Yet Rose noticed sadness about Harry as he said the words.

Rose shook her head, but she knew what Harry didn't. Her mother had poisoned her daughter against her. Taken her away and made her into a snooty, selfish woman like her. There was so much more to this story, but Rose couldn't continue.

"I'm sorry if I upset you, Harry," she said. "But it felt good getting it off my chest. I'd better go. It's getting late." She rose to leave.

"Here, Rose, take my Bible with you. Read it tonight, and

keep it for a bit. You may find some answers."

Rose took the Bible in her hands. The few passages Harry had read sounded hopeful and inspiring. Perhaps she would read a little.

When she arrived back at her own apartment, Rose turned in early. It had been a long day, and reliving the stabbing memories of Toni and Mama wore her out.

Chapter Three

*T*oni Warner brushed a lock of dark blonde hair from her eyes, squinting into her rearview mirror as she applied the finishing touch of lipstick to her full lips. Not bad for forty-one, she thought, while slipping the Gucci sunglasses onto her tan face. Her fingers undid another button on the silk blouse she wore, exposing a bit more skin. She turned into the traffic of downtown Pittsburgh, weaving in and out of the lanes with her most prized possession, her Mercedes.

It was going to be a great day. She'd just clinched the deal on an extremely huge merger between her advertising company, Harrison Bardwell, and The Fulton Corporation, an old rival. This would put her back on the map as one of the most prestigious executives in the area. Not bad for a single lady with drive and passion.

Toni's cell phone buzzed, and she reached for it on the passenger seat with a slender hand when her heart stopped for a moment. Mother! No, she wouldn't answer it. Too many good things were happening right now. No time for her mom's silly, idle chatter and guilt speeches. The four months her mother Rose had been away were the happiest in Toni's life. Not having to answer to her, look into her haunted eyes, watch her mother living like some sort of corpse. No, this was much better for them. She threw the cell phone back onto the passenger seat, cranking the volume of the satellite music in her car, drowning memories of her mother into precious oblivion.

Around six in the evening, Toni arrived at her apartment high above Mt. Washington in the Pittsburgh area. Throwing her keys into a brass key holder, she kicked off her high heels and walked over to the small, but well-stocked bar across the room. Pouring herself Glenlivet and tonic, she sat upon the leather sofa, legs curled under her, running her fingers over the rim of the glass. She smiled, proud of how she handled herself today in the office. She'd not only clinched the merger, but also had been responsible for the firing of Ben Stevens.

Toni thumbed through a few text messages from coworkers on her cell phone, deleting them one by one. Some of them were shocked, yet others applauded her bravery. Ben might be missed by a few. After all, he was a ladies man, handsome in an almost boyish way. Yet none of them knew him as she did, a young man who used any means, especially his charm, to climb the ranks, smothering each of them in the process to get what he wanted. He fancied himself an executive in the company, but instead he was a punk-nosed brat, barely thirty-years-old. He'd slept with some of the top-ranking higher-ups thinking it would propel him further than others who'd slaved for years, making the company the top advertising firm in the Tri- State area.

Toni had other reasons for disliking Ben. After all, though he'd been at least ten years her junior, they'd talked seriously about marriage at one point. With her youthful appearance, Toni could pass for a woman in her early thirties. Ben had been taken with her charm, elegance and brains, or so he said. He pledged his love to her one passionate evening, but when she'd found out about his other dalliances, Toni ordered him out of her apartment, throwing framed photos, vases and anything she could get her hands on at him. He'd left unwillingly, promising to change. It had been much too late and the damage was already done.

While she finished thumbing through her texts, the one missed call from the day appeared on her screen. Toni rolled her eyes thinking of her mother, a slight pang of guilt gnawing on her insides. She dismissed the feeling, drained the glass of amber liquid before her and then got up to pour another. After all, it had been almost four months since they'd spoken. Not like that was unusual for either of them. Toni remembered a time when they'd gone almost two years without talking.

Toni headed into the bedroom with her drink and set it

on her dresser. She slipped the silk blouse from her body and stared at herself in the mirror. I look like her, she thought, big brown almond-shaped eyes, high cheekbones, but I'm nothing like her.

Toni picked her drink back up and sat on the edge of her bed, sipping the scotch, enjoying the woody flavor. Though her stomach growled with hunger, she ignored the feeling and lay back upon the mountain of designer pillows on her bed. I miss Gram, she thought. Gram understood. I'm so like her.

My mother's a weak woman. Toni shivered thinking back to the first time she really understood this about her mom. It had been her fourth- grade year when one of the teachers in her school asked what hospital her mother was in and Toni had innocently answered, "Dixmont." The teacher had hushed Toni, and she hadn't understood what she'd said wrong.

Young Toni hadn't known what a state mental facility was. All she'd known was her mother had been acting odd, and then one day her daddy told her Mother was going to be away for a while. To a little girl, the words were scary, but Toni, even at her tender age, had hoped her mother would get better and act more like a mommy when she came home.

As time went by, the little girl began to understand. The stigma attached to mental illness and nervous breakdowns weren't something you talked about in polite company. Her mother had been in and out of hospitals several times, when

Toni's grandmother stepped in finally and began raising the girl.

Gram Ruth had been a soul mate and friend to her. Gram's elegant ways, exquisite home and expensive belongings showed Toni there was so much more to life than the prison world her mother lived in. Toni joined high society even as a teenager, and attended charm school and ballet classes. There wasn't anything Ruth would deny her only grandchild.

The buzz of the cell phone next to her on the bed brought Toni out of her reverie. Ben. She let it go to voicemail and thought about deleting it before listening to what he had to say.

Chapter Four

Abby Carson finished buckling baby Allison into the child safety seat of the minivan she drove while the fraternal twins Gavin and Nicholas, five, were old enough for the 'big kid' booster seats.

"Okay," she said, backing out of their driveway. "Today we're going to see Pap Pap. He's not in his house anymore, but he lives in a nice, new place. We're going to cheer him up guys and I want everyone to be on their best behavior." She steered into traffic from New Stanton, taking the turnpike which would head to Route 30, a straight shot into Ligonier where her father now lived.

"Momma," Nicholas, the talkative twin began. "Why couldn't Pap Pap stay with us?"

"Well, honey, for one thing, Pap can't walk the stairs anymore. Do you remember when he fell last year and how much he hurt? Well, we don't want that to happen again to him, right?" Abby glanced into her rearview mirror.

"Yeah, I guess," Nicholas said, prying a Transformer figure from his brother's hand. Gavin proceeded to shriek until Abby settled them both down again.

"That won't do, boys. We need to work on sharing, okay?" Abby watched as Nicholas handed the toy back to his brother.

A short time later, Abby pulled into a parking space at Huntington. The birds were especially musical on this Saturday afternoon. Though a few clouds dotted the blue sky, the day was warm and humid for early summer. She unbuckled the boys from the middle seats, climbing into the back of the van for the baby. Allison had fallen asleep on the short trip and looked groggily at her mother, a sweet grin breaking out onto her face.

Abby thought about her dad, and hoped he'd been getting along okay in the last three days. It was her first visit to him since she and her brothers had dropped him off. She wanted to make sure he saw his grandchildren as much as possible. The four of them knocked at his door and when Harry opened it, his face burst into a rapturous smile.

"Hello young'uns," he said, bending a little lower and scooping the twins into a hug. Squeals of delight came from Nicholas while Gavin wriggled out of his grandfather's arms. Baby Allison, wide awake now, reached two chubby arms toward her grandpa.

Harry straightened up, Nicholas clinging to his legs, and held out his arms for the baby. She went willingly to him, giggling at the silly faces he made.

"Well hi there, little lady," Harry made smooching noises at the baby in his arms. She touched his face with delicate little fingers, and gurgled a word that sounded strangely like "pap." Harry smiled and said, "That's my beautiful little Abby."

Abby winced. Dad had been calling baby Allison "Abby" a lot lately. Perhaps she reminded him of herself as a baby. But the thoughts of his "Old-Timers dementia," nagged at her. If he was losing a little more of his brain function, who knew how long until he might not even remember who they all were?

"Daddy, it's Allison," she corrected, laying a hand on his arm. "You called her Abby again."

Harry's face scrunched as if he was thinking hard about something. His cheeks reddened, and he said, "Well, I knew that."

"Come on, boys," Abby said, removing Nicholas from his grandfather's legs and taking Gavin by the hand. "Let's bring Pap Pap his presents, shall we?" Nicholas whooped with excitement and ran into the apartment before them.

"Let me show Pap, Mommy, let me," Nicholas whined. Gavin stood shyly off to the side, his thumb creeping toward his mouth.

"No," Abby said, "let's have Gavin give Pap his gift." She

motioned for her quieter son, and he beamed like the sun. "Here, Gavin, you bring this to Pap."

When they all were seated, Gavin brought his grandpa a brightly colored gift bag. Harry tried to hug him, but the little boy quickly ran back to his mother's side, shrieking.

"What's the matter with him?" Harry asked, digging past tufts of yellow and blue tissue paper.

"Well, I've been meaning to talk with you, Daddy. When we have a little privacy later, I need to tell you a few things." Abby sat back with the baby in her arms and Gavin wrapped around her legs. Nicholas, at his grandpa's side, tried to pull items from the bag.

"Well, lookie here," Harry said, retrieving boxes of puzzles from the bag. "The Eiffel Tower and the Statue of Liberty. Thank you all so much." Harry hugged the gifts to himself as if he thought someone would steal them away.

"Pap, can we open them, huh?" Nicholas bounced up and down in front of his grandpa, trying to snatch one of the boxes from the man's grip.

"Let's wait until Pap sets up shop on the kitchen table, alright buddy?" Harry said. "You guys hungry? I have a wonderful apple pie."

"Where'd you get that, Daddy?" Abby asked. She let Allison down onto the floor to crawl for a bit, but kept a close watch over her.

"My neighbor lady brought it to me a few days ago." Harry tapped his forehead with one hand. "I almost forgot, look at this lovely blanket she gave me." He scooped the burgundy afghan into his arms from behind the sofa.

Abby took the blanket, admiring the delicate lines of crocheting. The stitches were impeccable, the pattern, quite intricate. The woman who made this had talent.

"So you have a friend?" she asked her father.

"Well, yes, I guess you can say that."

"I'm glad for you, Daddy." Abby retrieved Allison before she pulled herself onto the coffee table, placing her gently on the floor, farthest from any other danger. A quick, loud protest emitted from the baby, and then she busied herself with her brother's shoelaces.

"How's Sean?" Harry asked.

Abby groaned inwardly. Had Daddy purposely not mentioned Tim, or was it his memory?

"He's good, Daddy. Timmy's doing well also." She watched her father's face for signs of recognition or indifference. Neither.

Just then, a knock sounded at the front door. Abby got up to answer, and as she opened the door, she was surprised to see Rose, the lady she'd met several days ago, standing there.

"Hello, Rose," Abby squeezed the woman in a warm embrace. "Wonderful to see you again." She motioned for

Rose to enter.

"I'm sorry, I didn't realize Harry had company," Rose said. "I was just returning his Bible. Perhaps I should leave."

"Nonsense, you come right on in," Harry said, getting up from the couch and wincing as arthritis popped in his knees. "I was just showing my family your lovely afghan."

"I'd love to learn how to crochet like that," Abby said. "I can only do a basic stitch. Would you be able to teach me sometime?"

"Oh, I'd love to," Rose said, entering the room.

"Come sit down and meet my grandchildren," Harry guided her to a place next to him on the sofa and took the Bible from her hands.

Abby watched as Rose sat, the look on her face priceless at seeing the small children in the room. It was a look of wonder, a look of almost rapture. Abby found herself liking this woman more and more.

"This is Nicholas," Harry pointed to one wiggly twin, "and, and. . ."

Abby saw her father's face cloud over, and realized he was having trouble with their names. She made the introductions and then scooped the baby up from the floor.

"May I hold her?" Rose asked. "I mean, if she'll come to me, that is."

"Yes, of course," Abby said, settling the baby onto Rose's

lap. "She's a good baby. She isn't very wary of people, though I wish she was."

Abby watched as Allison looked up into Rose's face. No sign of fear at sitting with a complete stranger.

"Well, if you'll all excuse me for a few minutes. I'd like to get lunch started," Abby said. "Just let me know if she gets fussy, Rose."

~*~

Rose held baby Allison on her lap. The little girl plucked at the locket Rose wore on the lapel of her blazer, making garbled baby sounds and smiling to herself.

"Why I guess you've made a little friend," Harry said, tickling his granddaughter.

Rose wrestled with the feelings inside her. Thoughts pummeled her, thoughts of her own little daughter at precisely the same age, and all the fears Rose had at that time. How she wished she'd been able to enjoy her baby more. But the fear of losing her had been too strong, the fear that somehow she, too, would be gone, just like the baby before her.

"She's a beauty," Rose said. The little girl curled into Rose's arms, her thumb slipping into her mouth. Rose rocked her gently.

When Abby walked back into the room and announced lunch was ready, Rose nodded toward the slumbering child in her arms.

"Here, let me take her, Rose," Abby said walking toward her.

"Oh, please," Rose whispered, "I'm fine, really. She's so beautiful. If you don't mind, I'd like to hold her."

"Aren't you hungry?" Harry asked, getting up slowly, his Bible clutched under his arm, as he headed toward the kitchenette.

"Actually, I'm not," Rose said. "You all go ahead."

After a few moments, Rose sat cuddling the baby in her arms alone in the room. The little chest rose and fell, the pink leotard and tutu she wore sparkled with fairy dust. The cream-colored skin smelled softly of baby powder, and her cheeks were rosy and healthy.

Rose felt a peace she hadn't known for the longest time. This baby, this miracle before her, a living, breathing realization of life and all that was good. She settled back into the cushions of the couch, little Allison stirring only a tiny bit as her thumb plopped from her mouth.

At least twenty minutes passed, Rose listening to the lively conversation coming from Harry's small kitchen. One of the little boys talked quite a bit, while the other seemed much quieter, she thought.

Abby peeked around a corner. "Rose, your arm must be killing you, please let me take her."

"I've not felt this happy in ages," Rose said.

"Well, then I'm going to impose just a bit more," Abby said. "I need to talk with my father about something. May I bring the boys in here? I'll put the television on with some cartoons. They have their toy bag too."

"That would be fine," Rose said. "You take whatever time you need with your dad."

The boys sat next to Rose on the sofa, their satchel of toys between them. Scooby Doo solved some type of mystery on the television and their rapt attention made Rose smile.

"Here, Rose. I've made you a sandwich." Abby laid a plate on the coffee table in front of Rose. "When Allison begins to stir, you call me, okay?"

Rose leaned forward, taking hold of the gooey grilled cheese sandwich with her free arm. She bit into it, the wonderful taste of sharp cheddar flooding her mouth. Abby had set a glass of apple juice next to the plate, and after a few more bites, Rose drank deeply of her glass.

"Daddy, I just need to talk to you for a few minutes in private." Abby held a terry cloth dishtowel in one hand and a dripping plate in the other. Harry sat at the table, his eyes never leaving her face.

While she continued drying the dish, Abby sighed. "Gavin was diagnosed with autism." There, it was out. The burden lifted, and she said it out loud. She'd finally come to terms with the word and all it implied.

Harry's face scrunched into a wrinkled frown. Not realizing that her father wouldn't understand the term, Abby told him a few facts.

"Tom and I knew something wasn't right. Nicholas has always been the more aggressive, the more vocal twin. But I started worrying that Gavin had some sort of developmental difficulty. He barely speaks, he wanders off, he sits for the longest time staring. I knew there was an issue. Tom and I took him to the pediatrician. He referred us to a specialist at Children's Hospital, and after a rigorous day of testing, they came back with the diagnosis."

"What does this mean for his future, Abby? Is there something they can do?"

"Yes, thankfully it's a mild form. They were surprised that nobody in the family exhibited any symptoms or had a diagnosis before."

Abby watched her father's face. Something registered, some type of emotion passed over it.

Harry blew out a long breath and ran his fingers through his short, gray hair. "Well, that's something," he said. "Are the doctors sure?"

"Yes, Daddy. We even had opinions from a few different doctors. It's a certainty." Abby finished drying the dishes as a torrent of tears began to flow from her eyes. Harry motioned for his daughter, arms extended and then gathered her into his arms.

"It's alright, it's okay," Harry crooned, almost rocking his daughter like a small child. Abby cried until she felt another tear couldn't possibly slip from her eyes.

"I'm sorry, Daddy. I didn't mean to upset you." She wiped her eyes while the tears began to subside and moved from her father's embrace. "It'll be fine, I know it will. God has been good to our family. Gavin's diagnosis isn't severe; it's a very mild form. It's just that, I knew something was wrong, and in some ways, it's such a relief to finally know."

"Yes, honey," Harry said, opening his Bible. "God will continue to be with us. We can count on it. Let's read a little."

Rose listened to the hushed voices in the kitchen, the baby beginning to stir. Clear blue eyes opened and looked into Rose's own. How much like her grandpa she looked, Rose thought. The baby didn't cry, just yawned and stretched out her arms, reaching toward her brothers.

How fortunate Harry is to have such love surrounding him. I'd give anything for Toni to pay me even a little bit of attention. I'd give anything to get a phone call from her.

Rose shook herself from her reverie as Allison squirmed on her lap, curious as to what her brothers were doing. The boys had set themselves on the floor, a coloring book open before them. Nicholas pulled large crayons from the box near him, intent on his work. Rose observed his determination to use the right colors for the pictures in the book, green grass, brown furry rabbit, yellow for the sun in the sky. Gavin seemed uninterested in what his brother was doing. He had a crayon in each hand and was busy turning them this way and that, content to study them. Rose placed Allison near the boys, but called out to Abby when the baby took a crayon and placed it in her mouth.

"I'm so sorry, Rose," Abby said, pulling the crayon from her daughter's grasp. "I didn't mean to leave you alone so long in here." Baby Allison wailed and reached for more crayons, kicking her little legs as her mother whisked her from the floor.

"No, honey, crayons aren't for eating," Abby crooned softly to her daughter, though the baby still fussed.

Rose watched Abby and for one guilt-ridden moment, wished she was her daughter. For one moment, she saw her life with a sweet girl like this, one who was soft spoken and kind. This beautiful woman before her appeared to be the epitome of gentleness. Rose chided herself for thinking such thoughts, remembering she did have a daughter, one she loved with her whole heart.

Harry stepped back into the living room. "My goodness," he said, "what's all the fuss?" He tugged playfully at the baby's small foot.

"Daddy, I think it's time for us to leave," Abby said. "Come on boys, let's give Pap a break. Let's clean up our toys." She sat on the floor spreading out a small, soft blanket for the baby to lie on. Changing her diaper while Allison thrashed around didn't appear to be an easy task. Yet Abby never raised her voice even once.

Rose stood from the couch, placed her hand at the small of her back and stretched. "I want to thank you for letting me hold your little one," she said to Abby. "You have lovely children. Thank you all for an enjoyable afternoon." Rose picked up her plate and glass to bring into the kitchen. Again, a feeling almost of envy stole through her, but was quickly replaced with happiness for her friend Harry. How good, how fortunate he was to have such love surrounding him.

When Rose walked back into the living room, Harry was saying goodbye to his grandchildren. Rose patted Allison's leg. "Beautiful little one," she said.

"Abby, what are your brother's names?" Rose asked, and saw Harry's face redden.

"Daddy, would you help me bring the baby's bag to the car?" Abby asked.

Harry picked up the vinyl satchel and reached for Gavin's small hand.

As he brushed past Rose and headed out the door, Abby reached out and touched Rose's arm. "Rose, in case you haven't noticed, my brothers are a source of discomfort for my dad. Maybe someday I can share some things with you, but that's for another time."

"I wish I'd never asked," Rose said. Her face flushed hot from embarrassment.

"No, oh, please don't say that." Abby said. "Everyone has a story, don't they? My father just chooses to handle some of his stories the wrong way." Abby took one last look around the room and motioned for Nicholas, who'd gotten involved in another Scooby Doo mystery that it was time to go.

"Their names are Sean and Tim, by the way," Allison said. "Timmy is the youngest in my family."

After Rose said her goodbyes, she walked the short distance to her own apartment thinking about the day's events. Everyone has a story, she mused. *Yes, I guess that's right.* In the few days she'd gotten to know Harry, he'd spoken to her about the man he once was. Could that be why he'd gotten so upset when she mentioned his sons? What could possibly have happened in that seemingly loving family?

Chapter Five

*T*im McMillen finished cutting the grass at his parent's house. He wiped the sweat from his forehead and the long hair from his eyes with the tail of the button down shirt he wore. Draining the can of Coors Light in a few swallows, he crumpled it and threw it into the metal trashcan near the shed he and his brother had built last summer.

He looked around the yard, his gaze falling on the place where their old fort had once stood, a huge, wooden structure their father constructed for them as children. Many days and nights of laughter and fun, protecting their sister Abby from invented foes. Late into the evening the neighborhood kids would leave one by one, while Tim and his big brother Sean would talk into the wee hours of the night. Their mom would find them curled up on blankets, shivering the next morning. Such good memories. Nothing remained of it now. Not one board.

Then his older brother Sean had gone off to college, his

sister following. Tim, the change-of-life child was left alone with older parents, an indifferent father and a saint for his mother.

Tim pulled another beer from the cooler sitting near the back deck. He popped the tab and swallowed a few gulps of the cold liquid. Placing the can on the side of his cheek, he squinted up into the sun, the rays of warmth engulfing him. His shirt plastered to his skin on the warm summer afternoon.

The realtor would be stopping by again with potential buyers later in the evening. He couldn't get rid of this house fast enough.

Of all his family, Tim was most able to keep up with jobs around the old homestead. His sister, Abby was married with three children, and Sean and his wife Becky were expecting their first child. Tim was a man alone, a man with too much time on his hands.

After draining the last of his can, Tim finished putting the Snapper in the shed along with other tools he'd used throughout the day. Surveying the yard, he nodded satisfactorily. Now to bag the debris. *If only I could pack up my debris.*

Tim's cell phone buzzed on the wooden stair of the deck where he'd laid it earlier. He walked over to glance at the caller's number.

"Hey, Ab, what's up?" Tim tucked the phone under his

chin while he scooped broken twigs and glass clippings into a black Hefty bag.

"Nothing much, Timmy," came the response. "I took the kids to see Daddy today." A small silence followed.

What did Abby want him to say? Oh, that's wonderful, how great. Oh, you're such a good daughter, kudos to you? Instead he found himself asking the question, the one that plagued him more and more. The one thought above all else as their father had aged, and it seemed nothing further could bother Tim.

"Did he ask about me at all?" Tim dropped onto the top step of the deck and closed his eyes waiting for the answer, knowing it already.

His sister's uncomfortable silence told him everything he needed to know. Another awkward pause followed.

"Uh, he's doing very well," Abby continued on the other end of the phone. "He made a friend."

Tim winced. "Hey, that's good," he said unconvincingly. "Sis, I gotta run, I'm busy out here in their back yard."

"Oh, I'm sorry, Tim. We can chat another time." Pause again. "You, uh, you okay?"

"Never better," Tim lied. "Thanks for asking."

"You want to come for dinner this weekend?" Abby pressed, her voice all sugar and sweetness.

"Nah, I'm still trying to update my resume'. I got a lot to

do." Tim blew breath out and clenched his right fist into a tight ball.

"Well, if you change your mind, I'm making pork tenderloin, your favorite, okay?"

"Sounds good. Thanks, sis, talk with ya soon." Tim pressed the button on his cell, ending the call. He sat back against the step, the hard wood digging into his back. Gripping the cell phone, he suppressed the urge to pitch it far across the yard.

A friend? Dad made a friend? Well, good for him. I bet it's a lady too, Tim thought. This time Tim did pitch the cell phone. It landed with a thump against the tree in the middle of the yard.

Womanizer, he thought. Stupid old man. Always the life of the party. Always the guy with the ladies swarming around him while his wife, the wallflower, sat quietly by.

Oh, I know all about you, Dad. I know what you did behind Mom's back.

Tim walked over to where his cell phone sat at the base of the old oak, the very tree that had been perfect for climbing when he was young. Birds sang in the branches above while he gathered the pieces of his new phone from the ground.

He pulled his pockets out, checking the right one first, then the left. A crumpled five dollar bill rewarded him. Another new phone would have to wait.

Tim looked at his watch. Five fifteen. Time to leave. He didn't want to be here when the realtor brought a happy family to *ooh* and *aah* over this house. Just sell the stupid thing so he could get back to his life.

Tim set the trash bags at the curb, and noticed something sticking from the mailbox at the front of the house. Some dumb new postal worker no doubt, not realizing the house was empty. Tim opened the flap of the mailbox and saw a flyer for an upcoming event at Trinity Episcopal, his parent's church. It was addressed to his father, good old Harry McMillen, the benefactor of the parish and longtime pastor of the church. Tim spat on the ground and crumpled the paper into a ball.

His sour mood was getting worse. He pulled the door open to his beat up Dodge truck, his mouth watering for another beer. Too bad he'd finished off his entire six pack this afternoon. Five bucks was enough for a few cans of the cheap stuff. Who cared that he didn't have anything to eat all day?

He spun the truck down the length of the driveway, peeling out onto the road past the well-manicured lawns and stately homes of Latrobe, Pennsylvania. How his parents were ever able to afford living here was beyond him.

Chapter Six

*R*ose sat in her favorite rocker, her foot keeping time to the classical music playing softly in the background. She looped her crocheting yarn over the hook, pulling tightly at the stitch, finishing another row of the baby afghan she was working on. Pinks and cream colors lay in a basket near her, colors chosen carefully for baby Allison. Rose hadn't forgotten the touch of the sleeping child. This blanket would be made with love for that beautiful little girl.

While a Strauss waltz reached its crescendo on the old stereo, Rose jumped when she heard a knock at her door. She chuckled, chiding herself for being so edgy. Another soft knock resounded and Rose called out, "Just a minute please." Putting the crocheting on the seat of the chair, Rose walked the few steps to the door.

Rose slid the chain, opening the door a crack to see who it was. Abby Carson's lovely face peered in at her.

"Abby, is something wrong?" Rose's heart skittered a few beats.

"No, Rose. I'm so sorry I didn't call first. I dropped some books off to my father this morning and wondered when I could have that crocheting lesson with you."

Rose slid the chain from the door, opening it widely to let Abby enter. The young woman was dressed in shorts and a t-shirt, but the impression of elegance surrounded her. Her auburn hair lay loosely about her shoulders, waves of it sticking up from the humidity no doubt.

"Well, why not start right now?" Rose asked. "I'm working on a little project and the stitch I'm using for this one is quite easy to follow. Come sit down." Just then Rose realized her baby doll was out. She had left it on the couch after retrieving it from the bedroom this morning. She felt her face grow hot.

"What a charming apartment you have," Abby said walking over to the hand-painted figurines gracing the corner cupboard. "These are so pretty." Abby viewed the paintings on the wall above.

"My goodness, these are very good." Abby's finger lightly traced the scribbled signature at the bottom right corner of the first portrait on the wall. In it was a young girl in a blue dress. She sat upon a wicker chair, a white cat curled at her feet.

"Thank you, dear. You're very sweet," Rose said. She moved several inches closer to her couch to try and snatch the doll. Perhaps she could toss it behind the couch, or cover it with another of her many blankets.

Just then Abby glanced over at her. "Oh." Her pretty smile beamed and she walked over to the sofa and picked the doll up. "I had one just like this when I was a little girl. My dad got it for me. How I loved her." Abby gently caressed Rose's vinyl baby, her long fingers trailing over the satin nightgown. "Thumbelina was her name, I think," Abby said.

Rose stood stock-still. Her heart hammered in her chest. Perhaps Abby was just being kind. Didn't she think it odd that an old woman had a dolly sleeping on her couch? She'd probably snicker behind her back later and even tell her brothers and Harry what a kook Rose was.

Abby laid the doll back. "This doll must mean something to you, Rose. You've taken very good care of her."

Rose watched Abby's face and realized the girl wasn't laughing at her. She breathed a slow breath out and softened.

"Yes, this doll was given to me by someone very special a long, long time ago. I guess she kind of keeps me company now, shall we say?" Changing the subject, Rose bade Abby to sit next to her on the other side of the couch. She pulled an extra crochet hook from her craft bag and an old ball of gray yarn.

"I won't need this yarn for anything," she said. "You can use it to practice. Here, let me show you."

Slowly and carefully Rose taught Abby the proper way to

begin a chain and from there, to start the next row. Fifteen minutes slipped into an hour.

"I never thought to ask you, honey, where are your children?"

"My husband's taking care of them today," Abby said. Her face was scrunched in determination as she clumsily slid the yarn from her hook. "I'm no good at this, Rose."

"You're doing fine. Keep practicing." Rose sat back on the sofa watching Abby. "You can take the ball of yarn home and work on it. Perhaps when you return next week, if you're visiting your father, I can check your progress, okay?"

"I'd like that," Abby said, laying down the yarn and crochet hook. She continued, "You're good for my father, you know," She looked Rose frankly in the eyes.

Rose looked down. "Oh, he's a sweet man. I'm lucky to know him. My goodness, it's only been a few weeks, but I feel sometimes I've known him much longer."

Abby laughed and patted Rose's knee. "He is a good man. I just wish my brothers got along with him better."

Rose opened her mouth to ask questions, but at the last moment, thought better of it. It was none of her business.

Abby rose and scooped up the ball of yarn, the crochet hook Rose had given her, and the small square she'd been working on.

"Rose, would you like to come to dinner sometime at my

house? I mean with my dad. I can pick you both up next weekend if you'd like."

Rose hadn't been out of this place in months. Well, maybe a doctor visit or two when the senior bus picked her up. "Yes, maybe I'll just take you up on that." They walked to the door. Abby turned just before she put her hand to the doorknob.

"Thank you for letting me barge in on your Saturday, Rose. I hadn't planned on staying so long, but this was very relaxing for me. I love your place. There's something so nostalgic about it to me. The paintings, the doll, the crocheting. I feel like I've stepped back in time while I'm with you."

"I hope that's a good thing," Rose said.

"Oh, yes, very much." Abby pecked Rose's cheek with her soft lips. "Thank you again, dear."

A little later, Rose stepped into her shower stall, letting the warm water cascade down her body. She felt a calmness she hadn't felt in a long time. She reviewed the afternoon visit with Harry's daughter. Abby was very special, a quick learner and such a tender-hearted person.

Rose thought about the Thumbelina doll. The one her favorite aunt had given her after the abortion. Abby had one like that too. Perhaps if Abby knew the circumstances surrounding the doll, she'd think differently about Rose. Thoughts of Skip, her first love, invaded Rose's mind. She remembered the time, the very last time she'd seen him.

Rose Whitaker lay shivering in her bed, the curtains drawn tightly against the sunshine of the day. This room is a prison, she thought. I'm not sure how much more I can take. She rolled over onto her side.

It had been two weeks. Two weeks since her mother had shamed her and now she continued her punishment locked in her room like some sort of criminal.

Rose had cried and cried until she felt she couldn't possibly shed another tear. She begged her father to just let her talk with Skip, let him know what had happened. But Papa's stoic silence and the fear in his eyes told Rose she'd never be allowed to see her beloved again.

Rose reviewed the events drawing up to her "bad day" as she called it. She'd been feeling poorly and had collapsed right before she and Skip were about to take a drive. She'd woken up in a hospital room, her mother accusing her of being some sort of loose girl. Rose loved Skip with all her heart. And she knew he loved her too. Many a night they'd talked late into the darkness as the stars began to come out, declaring their feelings for one another. Though Skip had a reputation, though he'd been booted out of the last school he'd attended, he'd changed. Rose saw his transformation before her eyes. The steely edge he'd had when they first met, melted as he saw more and more of Rose. Yet Rose's mother always treated him as if he was a dangerous insect, watching him, waiting to pounce on his every word. Correcting his grammar, scolding him for his manners. Rose couldn't stand how harshly Mother spoke with Skip.

Mother envisioned Rose as a debutante, a young lady with a promising future, a future which involved marrying into wealth and power.

Rose hated her stuffy world. She despised the hours of piano lessons, the ballet, all of it, just a sham to her. Rose wanted nothing more than to be married someday to a man she loved with her whole heart and soul. And she wanted children, lots and lots of children. She'd never be the kind of mom her mother was. She'd never force a child into a mold she wasn't meant to become.

Rose pushed the covers from her body and swung herself out of bed. A hollow ache lay within her, whether it was physical or in her soul, she wasn't sure. Rose tentatively took a step and felt her legs give way beneath her. She landed softly on the carpet, burying her head in her hands, sobs racking her body once again.

A baby. Her baby. How could Mother have made her do such a thing? It hurt so much, the realization of what she'd gone through. Shame and guilt covered Rose, suffocating her. Thoughts pummeled Rose's mind, thoughts of intimacy with Skip. Good girls didn't do this sort of thing, especially when the consequences were so high. She'd been responsible for the taking of a life. This thought above all else haunted Rose whether she was awake or asleep, fragments of nightmares from the last week, darkness, a valley with small bodies lying amidst the cold, dark earth.

Nathaniel. Rose spoke the name in the quietness of her tortured soul. Though she hadn't known if the baby would have been a boy or a girl, Rose felt the presence of a little boy. She clutched her stomach and rolled herself into a fetal position on the carpet, rational thought trickling away.

She'd heard a knock at the front door just then, a pounding, booming sort of hammering and raised voices. Rose drew herself from the floor, trudging to the window and opened it a crack to hear better.

What she'd heard made her heart stop. It was Skip! He'd come to see her. Come to talk with Mother and Father. Rose listened as Papa and Skip spoke on the porch beneath her window. She couldn't hear much, though she heard her name in harsh tones several times. Maybe only a few moments passed, but Rose saw her beloved walking away from the house, head down, dejected. She heard the front door slam beneath her while she clutched the window sill. Opening the window a bit higher she screamed out.

Skip turned to the sound and saw Rose in the window. The haunted, sick look on his face spoke volumes. He carried a large package under his arm wrapped in brown paper. He stared at Rose from across the yard and shrugged his shoulders slightly. "I'm so sorry, Rose," he called to her. He turned away and continued walking to his pickup truck. Rose watched as he threw the package into the back, hopped into his vehicle and peeled away in a loud squeal of tires and smoke.

Gone, just like that, gone. Rose sank to the seat of her vanity table, head in her hands. Her tears, a hot torrent of pain poured forth from her, the ache within, alive and real. She knew she'd never see Skip again.

As summer turned to fall, Rose's parents enrolled her in a Catholic boarding school. She was forced to wear a daily uniform for her senior year. Forced to endure the elderly nuns with their sour faces, sour manner and clucking tongues. She'd been picked on for every little thing she said.

Nuns with their angry voices and accusing stares. Rose never felt so alone.

As soon as graduation rolled around, Rose's parents shipped her off to Aunt Hilda's house in Boston. It was under her aunt's watchful eye that Rose would learn more about herself than ever before. Though Hilda was a coarse, old spinster, she took to Rose, showing her the art of cooking, crocheting and homemaking. It was here, with her father's older sister, Rose would have some of her fondest memories. It was here she would meet the man she'd eventually marry.

Life would settle into a routine for Rose and thoughts of Skip and their baby would eventually fade only to resurface when she found herself expecting once again.

Enough. Rose shut the water of her shower, standing for a moment shivering as the chill of the air hit her body. She reached for the towel which lay atop the commode and wrapped it around herself. It was all a long, long time ago.

Chapter Seven

*T*oni Warner cursed herself for allowing Ben to speak. She sat across from him at L'Elegante Restaurant smoldering in anger while he continued flattering her. Did he think this would bring his job back? She silently cursed again over her decision to even join him tonight. Somehow he'd managed to coerce her into meeting him, and in her loneliness, she'd agreed.

Piano music played softly in the background of the five-star restaurant. They sat near a huge window overlooking downtown Pittsburgh. The twinkling lights of the city flared golden in the distance.

"So anyway, I'm glad to have a fresh start, a clean slate, honey," Ben said, sitting back in the booth of the lowly lit restaurant. His Gucci suit looked amazing on him, and he'd removed his tie during the evening and unbuttoned the top two buttons revealing his tan chest. He ran his hands through his dark hair, and his deep brown eyes felt as if they were prying into her soul.

"Don't you "honey" me, you arrogant, egotistical . . ." Toni's fingernails dug into her hands underneath the tablecloth.

Ben cut her off. "Listen, I'm sorry. I've told you time and again just how much. I was a fool for the mistakes I made at the company. I'm just a little boy." He winked at her, his full lower lip pouting.

Toni wriggled uncomfortably. He was doing it again. Ben could turn the charm on and Toni would feel herself flushing with excitement. She drained the glass of white wine before her and motioned to the maître d for another.

Ben slid his hand across the table, prying Toni's fingers from the empty glass. He stroked her hand with his thumb. "Toni, I've known since I moved to this area how strongly I feel about you. I was stupid and dumb and acted on selfish impulses." He came around to her side of the booth, slipping in beside her.

Toni scowled and pulled away, scrunching herself as far into the corner as she could. Ben slid nearer to her and turned her face to him, his warm, strong hands on either side. "You look at me, Toni Warner. I should hate you and never speak with you again after what you did. I wanted to meet with you tonight to tell you how sorry I am and how much I really care about you." He kissed her then, a long, slow kiss.

Toni's hard exterior cracked. She hated herself as tears

welled up and a trail of them trickled down her cheeks. She brushed them away and closed her eyes.

"You don't understand what I'm going through," she said, opening her eyes, pushing his hands away and looking straight at Ben. He pulled a silk handkerchief from his pocket and dabbed tenderly at her cheeks.

"Then tell me," he said, looking at her in that frank way of his. "Please tell me what's going on."

The waiter brought two glasses of wine and laid them down. "May I get anything else for you, Ms. Warner?"

"No, Harold. We're fine. Just some privacy."

"Very good, Madame. Please signal if you would like something."

Taking a deep breath and a sip of Sauvignon Blanc, Toni relaxed in her seat. "Sometimes I feel like the loneliest person on the face of the earth," she said. The tears began to subside and Toni pulled out a small, gold compact. Satisfied she hadn't cried her eye makeup completely off, she shut the case and smiled a small, tired smile.

"I feel so misunderstood. I'm a woman, I'm successful, I'm very confident, and those things make me a monster. Nobody really knows me. . ." Toni trailed off. She laughed, but it was cold and without humor. "The only person was my Gram Ruth and she's been gone for years now. My mother and I don't even speak."

"Toni, why don't you talk to your mom? It isn't like she doesn't try to talk with you."

Toni winced inwardly. Yes, Ben was right. Mother used to phone her every two days for the longest time. Now it was only once every couple weeks. Toni couldn't bear the thought of talking with her, yet she longed for family, any family.

Toni watched Ben's face and body language. Should she open up to this man, this man who'd hurt her so grievously recently? He was all she really had.

"Ben, did I ever tell you my mother was hospitalized when I was growing up?"

Ben shook his head and moved closer. He grabbed Toni's hand and held on. "I can tell you need to talk about this. Please trust me this time. I don't know what else I can say. I came tonight to make peace with you. Show me that same courtesy. I'm here for you."

Though Toni wrestled with her thoughts, though everything inside her screamed how wrong this all was, she felt herself melting into the moment, into those deep brown eyes of Ben's.

"When I was in fourth grade," she began with a small shudder, "I came home from school one day to an empty house. I thought something bad happened to my mom because she was always there for me. The worst part was I'd noticed she wasn't herself for a while before this, but I never understood why. I remembered my father's work number and called him. His office told me he'd been gone for hours. Then I really panicked.

"Mom had anxiety issues, you see. She had an unnatural fear for me when I'd go play with friends. She made me check in with her at least every half hour or so. She fretted about me to an obsessive point, but on this day, she wasn't even there." Here Toni stopped and took another sip of wine, swilling it in her mouth, letting it cleanse the taste of bitterness from her.

Ben picked her hand up and kissed it softly. "Go ahead," he urged.

"I sat alone in my house for over an hour that day, crying. My father came home then and told me Mom wasn't well and she'd be away in a hospital for a bit. When I asked why, he couldn't answer me. And when I asked which hospital and he told me Dixmont, I had no idea it was a state mental facility. I had no idea the magnitude of my mother's problems. Dad wouldn't elaborate, and after a time, Gram Ruth came and took me to live with her. I hated my mother during that whole while. She never called, never asked to see me in the whole six months she was gone that first time."

Toni sighed, blowing a long breath from her lungs, pushing away the feelings which were all too raw once again.

"I'm so sorry," Ben said. "I had no idea."

"Oh, there were other times too, but by then, I'd been

staying with my grandma so long, it didn't matter to me anymore. My gram and I became very close. She was my whole world, I guess."

"Did you ever find a diagnosis about your mom?"

"I was told her type of mental issues aren't something that runs in families. It's more of a situational thing, like a traumatic incident triggered something. At least that's what I learned as I became a little older."

"Surely you and your mom got along after that. I mean, you were her daughter for goodness sakes. She couldn't have been hospitalized all her life."

"We never got along after that, and if you think I'm like her, you're as crazy as she is," Toni snapped.

"Oh, no, Toni, I would never suggest that." Ben sat back and crossed his arms in front of himself. He had a faraway look in his eyes that made Toni uncomfortable.

Here, Toni paused, excusing herself from the booth. She headed to the ladies' room and waited while an older woman washed her hands and checked her makeup for what felt like an eternity. When the woman left, and Toni was alone in the room, she held onto the counter, shaking whether with fear or rage, she wasn't sure. She pulled out a small container from her purse and popped a tiny pill into her mouth, swallowing it with water in her hand cupped under the faucet. She straightened her wraparound shawl and smoothed her black crepe dress.

After taking a few deep breaths, she rejoined Ben at their table.

Ben had taken the liberty of ordering after-dinner liquors. He tipped his glass to Toni and together they sipped the amber liquid. Toni decided not to speak any more about her mother.

"I have an interview Tomorrow at Berkely and Shaw," Ben said, after a long pause. "I think it will be a nice change for me. I'm pretty much a shoe-in to get it with the experience I have."

Toni turned toward Ben. "Huh. Well, that's good for you. I wish you luck." Her mind was still in the past. *Maybe there is something wrong with me. I'm sitting here with a man I'm responsible for firing, I'm totally attracted to him, and I'm fretting over my loony mother.*

"Ben, I don't want to be alone tonight. I don't think I can bear it. Would you, just for this evening please stay with me?"

Ben signaled the waiter for his check. "Now you're talking. Come on, let's get out of here."

Chapter Eight

Rose and Harry sat together in the dining area of Huntington. Even in the crowded room, Rose focused on Harry as if he was the only person there. His charm and wit warmed her as he told story after story of his schooldays. She wiped her eyes with the napkin in her lap as another fit of giggles caught her.

"I swear, Harry, you're the silliest man I've ever known. I can't believe you did that to the poor teacher."

"Well, Rose, I was what they called a juvenile delinquent back in my time, I guess you'd say. It was my idea to change the desks around in the room before old lady Watkins came back in. The other kids just followed my lead."

Rose took a bite of the egg salad sandwich on her plate and then shook her head. A rumble of thunder sounded overhead followed by a brilliant flash of lightning.

"Ooh, that was close," she said. "I'm not too crazy about storms."

"How about you, Rose? Didn't you ever just once get

yourself into a little mischief in school? Don't tell me you were one of those good girl types. I can see a twinkle in your eyes, young lady."

"Oh pish posh, I never got into trouble. I had a strict mother and I was always afraid of angering her. My brother, William was the bad one. He was caught smoking when he was eleven, drinking when he was fifteen. My parents had a real time of it with him."

"I was an only child for the longest time. Then I found out I had a brother, well, half-brother," Harry said, pulling the crust from his bread and sticking it into his shirt pocket.

"What on earth are you going to do with that bread?"

"I feed the birds in my yard, you see. Poor little creatures. I've wanted to ask if they'll get a couple birdfeeders around this place for them. Especially in the winter, it'll be hard for them to find food."

"That's sweet of you. Here, take my crusts too." Rose peeled the remaining bit of her sandwich apart and handed the pieces to Harry. She picked up the container of chocolate pudding, stirring it with a plastic spoon.

"I love the birds," Harry said as another boom of thunder resounded outside the building. Rain began to fall, at first lightly, and then it came pelting down with torrential force.

"Goodness, would you look at that?" Rose stared out the window and shuddered. The day turned gray and the rain fell in sheets outside the windows of the dining area. Some residents began to stir, pulling out umbrellas and rain gear.

"Oh, a little rain never hurt anything. As a matter of fact, it's good for us. It's good for our plants."

"Well, it's not too good for our arthritis," Rose said, wincing as she stretched in her chair. "I can feel my joints stiffening." Another crack of lightning and thunder rattled the panes of the windows. Rose put her spoon down, her hand trembling.

"Rose, just look at you. Why, you're scared to death," Harry said. He moved closer to her and put her sweater about her shoulders, his hand resting lightly on her back as the tremors subsided.

"Aw, that was sweet of you, Harry. I've been terrified of storms since I was a young girl. I'm sorry, what were we talking about?"

Harry rubbed Rose's shoulder gently while he continued speaking. "I had a huge garden many years ago," he said with a faraway look in his eyes. "I canned tomatoes, made pickles, jarred up peppers. Yeah, it was a real nice one."

"Did your wife help?"

"No, she was so involved in our church with ladies' guilds and all those important things a pastor's wife does. I usually had kitchen duty."

"Excuse me, Harry, but did you say Pastor's wife?"

Harry chuckled and tugged at the neckline of his sweater as if some invisible clerical collar was still there. "Yes, I guess I never told you, did I? My wife and I were the elders at Trinity Episcopal in Latrobe. I was pastor there for well over twenty years."

Rose stared as if she was struck. Harry was a man of God?

"Rose, you look at me like I'm contagious or something. Have I said something wrong?" Harry scratched his silver white hair.

Rose backed up from the table. "No, I, uh, I guess I felt you were a little more like me."

"What on earth does that mean? I'm no different from you."

"Oh, but you are, Harry. I'm, well, I'm not much for religion. I had it shoved down my throat as a young girl, and I don't care for the phonies and hypocrites."

Harry tried reaching for Rose's hand. "You're wrong, you know. I'm not religious or whatever you call it. I had the calling as a young man to do good with my life. After all I'd done as a wild teenager, I knew I needed to make a difference in this world. That was just how I'd chosen to do it. But I'm no better than anyone." Harry pulled his hand away from Rose and hung his head. "Someday, perhaps I'll share stories with you. I'm afraid I was a miserable failure at times."

Rose's heart melted. That this man could open up so frankly before her. Harry was genuine, if nothing else.

"I just remembered," Rose said. "Abby invited me for dinner next week with you to her house. I hope you don't mind."

Harry's blue eyes twinkled in a handsome face. "Actually I'd love that."

~*~

Rose picked up her glass of wine, a fit of giggles overtaking her once again from the stories Harry and Abby talked about. The children were napping, and they all sat on the screened-in porch at the side of Abby's house. Abby's husband Tom was a delightful man, and kept trying to refill Rose's glass from the bottle of red wine he held in his hand.

"No, Tom, I'm fine. I was never one for much drinking," Rose said. "You're trying to get me drunk and then I'll really start carrying on."

Tom Carson, a short man, had a huge, booming voice which made up for his small stature. Good-natured and a bit talkative, he'd put Rose at ease from the minute she and Harry walked through the door.

Harry's son Sean and his quiet wife Becky sat together on the other side of the table with Sean constantly attentive to his pregnant wife.

"Now that's something I'd really like to see," Tom

laughed. "Come on, Harry, let's show her how a real Irishman drinks."

Harry covered his own glass with his hand. "No, I'm good. I get heartburn from wine now. You have another one for me."

"Don't mind if I do." Tom poured himself a glass from the dark burgundy bottle.

Hearty laughter filled the air.

Abby got up to clear plates and Becky slid out of her chair to help. Rose found herself liking each member of this family. Their closeness and the way they spoke to one another showed her something that had been lacking for the longest time in her own life.

"Here, let me help too," Rose said, gathering a few of the forks and spoons and followed the women into the house.

Abby's little boy, Gavin, walked into the kitchen rubbing the sleep from his eyes.

"You hungry, Bud?" Abby asked, going over to him and picking him up.

Rose watched the way Abby acted with the little boy. She'd found out earlier today that he had a form of autism. It didn't seem to affect the family in a negative way, and they treated him no differently. As a matter of fact, they treated each child the same with no favoritism.

"Is your brother up yet?" Abby asked.

Gavin shook his blonde head and motioned to the counter where several desserts sat uncovered.

"No, honey, those are for later. Let's get you some chicken fingers or hot dogs, okay?"

Gavin shrieked and began thrashing in his mother's arms. Nicholas, the other twin, walked into the room then.

"Come on. Let's see if Daddy will help us out." Abby walked over to the door with Gavin still fussing in her arms. Becky, her sister-in-law, called out to Tom.

"Hey, whoa, what do we have here?" Tom entered the house, pulled Gavin from his wife and took him into the living room, speaking in comforting hushed tones. After a few minutes, the boy settled down.

Nicholas seated himself at the kitchen table, a matchbox car in either hand while he raced them back and forth.

"Rose and Becky, would you girls mind heating a few things in the microwave for the boys while I check on Allison? I'm sure she's up by now too. Thanks so much." Abby excused herself from the room.

Becky hardly spoke a word as she scooped potatoes, hot dogs, chicken and corn into small plates. Rose decided it was best to begin loading the dishwasher, and also made a sink full of sudsy water to wash some of the bigger pots and pans.

"When is the baby due?" Rose asked.

"I have about another three months to go. We're really

excited," Becky offered in her quiet little voice.

"Yes, my goodness, that's wonderful." Rose scrubbed at a cast iron skillet with a steel wool pad, enjoying the usefulness, the camaraderie with these people.

"This is a very nice family," Rose said while picking at caked-on cheese. She gave up after a moment and decided to soak the pan. While wiping her hands on the dish towel, she saw another car pull up outside the house.

"Oh yes, I just love them," Becky said, and put some plates piled high with food on the table.

Nicholas put his cars aside and grabbed a piece of chicken. Tom walked back in with Gavin just then and the three of them sat together.

"Tom, I can't thank you enough for inviting me over today. I was just telling Becky how sweet you all are. It's been such a long time since I was around a big family like yours."

"It's been my distinct pleasure having you here today, Rose," Tom said while helping his boys cut their hotdogs. "I'm glad you and Harry met one another. You two seem good together."

Rose felt herself blushing. She sat at the other chair. "I was surprised to find out Harry's a former pastor."

Tom laughed. "Yeah, I guess they're just down-to-earth folks. I felt uncomfortable myself at first when I met Abby. I wondered if her dad was going to watch every move I made. I was afraid I'd have to watch everything I said. But Harry's nothing like that. We got along well from the start." Here Tom stopped for a minute. "We even used to enjoy having a couple drinks together."

Abby walked into the room, baby Allison in her arms. The baby was dressed in a yellow sun outfit. It lit her face up like an angel, Rose thought. Allison wriggled to get down from her mother and climbed into her daddy's lap to sit with him.

"My gosh, these children have good appetites," Rose remarked.

"Tom, who's out there on the porch with Daddy and Sean?"

"Oh, sorry, honey, I didn't know anyone else was here."

Becky spoke up then. "It's Tim. I think he's brought someone with him." Her voice sounded flat, emotionless.

Abby's face lit up. "Excuse me, everyone." She practically tripped over her feet to get out the door.

"Let's hope this goes well," Tom said. "I told her maybe she should have invited Tim another time."

Rose felt confused. Abby seemed ecstatic at her younger brother's arrival. But the way Becky and Tom looked at one another told another story.

~*~

Shock was the only word Abby would use later to describe how she felt when she went out to greet her brother,

Tim. He stood by the entrance of the porch, arms crossed tightly before him, rumpled t-shirt on his scrawny frame, several days' growth of beard stubble on his chin and greasy, unwashed hair. Though it had only been a few weeks since she'd seen him, he looked so different, so lost. An extremely young-looking blonde stood next to him in skintight, short clothing.

"Timmy!" Abby ran to her brother, hugging him as tightly as she could. "It's so good to see you." Tim stood stiffly by, not even bothering to return the hug his sister gave him. He stared past his sister toward the figure of their father sitting at the table on the porch. Their brother Sean had risen from the table and came toward his siblings. He extended his hand in a warm handshake.

"Good to see you, bro," Sean said, clapping his brother heartily on the back. "Come on, sit down, have something to eat."

"This is Crystal," Tim finally said as he put a hand onto the young girl's shoulder in introduction.

"Welcome, Crystal," Abby said, giving the girl a hug, smelling stale smoke. "We have plenty left to eat. Everything's in the house." Abby said a silent prayer. Would her brother and father speak to one another?

Harry, who'd been sitting quietly through this scene, squinted a bit at the figure of his youngest son. His face scrunched like it did when he was trying to retrieve a memory, Abby thought.

"Richard?" he asked. Then the fog seemed to lift from his eyes and he murmured a polite "hello."

What was it with Dad, Abby wondered? What made him think of Timmy as Uncle Richard? Perhaps their uncle had resembled Tim at the same age or something. At any rate, it was unnerving, and it bothered Abby that sometimes Harry didn't seem to realize he had a younger son.

Abby ushered Tim and Crystal into her house. She looked back at her father and he'd risen from the table. "Daddy, can I get you something?"

"No, I just need the bathroom's all," Harry said, pausing a moment to straighten up his body. He entered the kitchen where everyone else stood and saw his grandchildren at the table.

"Hey, there's my wee ones," he said, bending down to plant a kiss atop Allison's little head. He ruffled the hair of the boys. "Pap will be right back." He shuffled out of the room.

"Rose, this is my other brother Timmy," Abby said, walking Tim over to the table where Rose sat. Not even making eye contact, Tim murmured a quick "hello" while Rose sat looking a bit perplexed.

Tom looked up at his wife and shook his head. Then to Tim he said, "Can I get you a beer?"

Abby felt heat rise up within herself. The last thing she wanted to serve her brother was alcohol. She'd smelled it on him earlier when she hugged him. Tim apparently had been drinking already today.

The sound of a crash from somewhere inside the house broke the tension of the moment. Tom handed the children to Abby and went to investigate.

Abby heard Tom's voice, the concern, almost on the verge of panic. "Pop, are you alright? What happened?" Abby left the children with the others and ran into the living room. She saw her father half-sitting on the floor, rubbing the side of his head.

"Daddy! My goodness!" She ran to her father. A small cut bled on Harry's forehead, his hands shook as he tried getting to his feet. "No, wait, Daddy." Abby put a hand against her father's chest while Sean ran into the room followed by Becky and Rose.

"I'm alright," Harry said. "Stop fussing over me. I tripped over a toy or something. That's all." He pushed his son and son-in-law away and after a moment, got to his feet himself.

Abby looked around. There was no toy on the ground, nothing he could have tripped on.

"I was trying to find the bathroom," Harry said. "What'd you people do, move it?"

Abby looked over at her husband. Tom pointed past

them at the far end of the room. "Powder room's in there, Pop. You sure you're okay?" Tom stood close to his father-in-law in case he wavered again. Harry swerved a bit unsteadily as he walked away muttering under his breath.

"He's got to start using a cane," Sean said quietly. "This is getting scary, Sis."

"I agree, but he gets so upset with me whenever I bring it up," Abby said. She looked over at Rose then.

"Rose, would you mind talking with my father about the benefits of walking with a cane? I notice you don't need one, but perhaps you have a way with him that some of us don't. He's quite hard-headed as you know." Abby brushed her long auburn bangs from her face while watching for her dad.

"Of course, dear," Rose agreed. "I'll try to speak with him tomorrow about it. He's a bit embarrassed, I think. Seems your daddy's a very proud man."

"You have no idea," Abby offered.

When Harry was through in the bathroom he saw his family and Rose still clustered in the living area and announced he was ready to leave. "I don't need all this attention," he grumped. "Time for us to go back home, Rose."

Tim, who had never left the kitchen to check on all the commotion, sat with his baby niece and little nephews. As she walked back into the room Abby observed how good Tim was with the children. It warmed her to see him actually smiling.

The kids seemed to adore him. Even Crystal who sat next to him spoke kindly to baby Allison.

"Thank you both for watching out for them. Dad's okay." She looked at Tim's face to see what might register there. Nothing. It was as if her brother didn't even care.

When Harry walked back through the kitchen to leave, he stopped and stared at his son sitting at the table. What felt like an eternity passed as father and son looked at one another, neither speaking.

Rose fell in quickly behind him as Tom placed her sweater about her shoulders. "Nice to have met you, Tim," she said smiling sweetly at him.

Tim glared at her. "Yeah, sure," he finally said.

~*~

"What is wrong with you?" Sean asked his brother a little later in the day. "Why do you always have to cop an attitude with the old man?"

Tim drained the beer sitting in front of him. Crystal sat at his side on the porch making little patterns with her long fingernails on his arm.

"Oh yeah, Sean, that's right," Tim's voice rose. "Everything's perfect between you and him now, huh?" Tim stood then, veins popping in his neck and he slammed a fist on the table causing Crystal to jump.

"We have no father!" Tim screamed. "We have a shell of

a man who never was a good father! It's worse than ever! He doesn't even see me when he looks at me!" Tim ran his hands through greasy hair. "He thinks I'm his brother, for crying out loud!"

The other family members were still indoors. Tim, Sean and Crystal had come out to the porch after Harry and Rose had gone. It wasn't going to work. Tim knew he didn't belong here.

"Timmy," Sean softened, "I came to grips last year with who he is. I think he tried the best he could while we were growing up. I didn't always see eye to eye with him, you know. But he's just an old man now. Maybe it's time for us to let it go."

"Count me out, bro," Tim said, grabbing Crystal's arm and pulling her from the table. "I should never have come here today. Abby, with her goody-good routine, always trying to fix someone. I'm not the one who's broken. Maybe our dad should have cared more a long time ago. Maybe he should have realized what a wonderful woman he had at his side with our mother instead of chasing every skirt in front of him!"

Abby came out onto the porch just then. "What's the matter? You're not going, Tim, are you?"

"Stop it, Ab, just stop it," Tim said. "Stop trying to repair me and please stop trying to force me and your stupid father to be nice to each other. He's dead to me. He died a long time ago when he cheated on Mom."

Abby winced as if struck. She reached a hand out to her brother but he slapped it away. "Just leave me alone, all of you." Tim screamed while pushing Crystal into his truck. He revved the motor and pulled quickly out from the front of the house, a trail of smoke in his wake.

Chapter Nine

Rose dabbed at the open cut on Harry's face with peroxide on a cotton ball from her small medicine chest. When Tom dropped them off, she persuaded Harry to come into her apartment for a moment. He winced as she pressed a bit harder.

"That smarts a bit, dear," Harry said, pushing at Rose's hand.

"I don't care," Rose said. "It needs attention." They sat closely together on the small loveseat in her living area. Harry reached out and cupped Rose's face gently with one hand.

"What on earth?" Rose asked as he bent his mouth toward hers and gave her a soft kiss.

"That's for you, sweetheart. I appreciate your care." Harry looked frankly into Rose's eyes as she felt herself blush and tried to look away from him.

"I'm serious, Rose. I'm so fortunate to have met you. I never dreamed I'd find love again in my golden years."

"Harry, you're a silly old man. You must have bumped

your head harder than I thought," Rose chuckled. Yet she allowed him to kiss her once again.

They sat back while Buttons the cat weaved in and out of their feet. It was the first time Harry had been in her apartment.

"I loved Julie with my whole heart," Harry said, reaching out to stroke Buttons. "She was a good woman. Good enough to put up with my antics, that is."

"I was in love a long time ago," Rose said. "When I was a teenager, I knew what true love was like. My husband was good to me, and I did care for him, but I don't think I ever was able to give my heart away like I did when I was seventeen."

Harry reached for Rose's hand and squeezed it gently. Looking up, he saw the artwork gracing her walls. "My goodness. You certainly have quite a few good paintings." He struggled to his feet, pulling Rose up with him. They walked arm in arm over to the wall filled with canvases.

"My husband bought me many of these throughout our marriage. He knew I loved watercolor paintings. I used to dabble in it a bit when I was a young girl, but never took myself serious enough."

"Well, these are very good. Any famous artists?" Harry traced his finger over the picture of the young girl sitting with her cat.

"No, I don't think anybody was well-known. That one in

particular was a gift given to me many, many years ago." Rose sighed.

"I never had talent like that," Harry said. "My brother, Richard was the creative one in our family. He could draw things, well, people from memory sometimes. He used to make us laugh with caricature sketches of people we knew." Now it was Harry who sighed.

"I miss him. He was a good man. . . troubled a bit, but we were very close."

"Come on, let's get a cup of tea and some cookies, shall we?" Rose asked and led Harry into her kitchen.

After they were seated at the table, Rose asked, "Tell me about your life, Harry, I mean growing up with your brother and all."

With steaming mugs of tea before them, Harry opened up. He picked at a lemon cookie first, breaking it in two and dipping one of the halves into his tea.

"My family lived in Avalon," Harry began. "Father was a railroad man. He was on the road quite a bit, sometimes gone for weeks at a time with the job he had as brakeman." Harry took another bite of cookie, chewing quietly, a faraway look in his eyes.

"They were a good couple, no screaming battles or anything like that. I was an only child for years until I found out I had a brother." Here, Harry paused as if to collect his thoughts. Rose sat quietly, waiting for him to continue.

"My mother had started digging through Father's pockets one time when he was away on a job. She found a picture of a really pretty young woman and a little boy. It confused her as you can imagine. What on earth was this doing in her husband's pocket? The worst part was what was written on the back of the picture though. It said: To my beloved, our son, Richard.

When Father returned from a two-week run, my mother was waiting in the sitting room of our home. She'd cried for days and when I asked her what happened, she wouldn't answer. I was about six years old at the time, I think.

Anyway, the screaming I'd never heard in all my childhood began that night. Through closed doors I heard Father try to comfort my mother. I heard her crying and saying the most horrible things imaginable to him.

After a few days, Father sat me down and explained to me he had another child. I was very confused as I was only a little boy myself. I didn't understand what that meant, you see. I thought my mom had another baby with him. It seemed though, that he had a completely different family. He'd met a woman when his job took him to Indiana, and in his loneliness he'd befriended her, and she helped him pass the time in more ways than one." Here Harry cleared his throat, looking uncomfortable.

"Please go on," Rose urged. She slid her hand across the table and covered Harry's hand with her own, gently squeezing it as if to reassure him.

"Well, time went on," Harry continued, "and the lady died. Her name was Angela, and she'd been quite sick and frail for a while. She'd contracted pneumonia and passed away while her son, Richard, was only nine years old. By that time, I was ten, so my half-brother was only a year younger than me, you see.

"Though it was hard for my mother, we moved Richard in with us. At first I hated him. I hated everything he stood for, my father's affair and double life. And all the pain he and his mother had caused my mother. We fought constantly, he was bigger than me, and I had to always try and prove myself to him.

"Then one day came when I was about fourteen or so. Richard had gotten into some trouble in school, and he'd come to me to help him out, confided in me. I was already a rascal myself, so the two of us bonded over our delinquency, I guess you could say. As the years passed, we grew much closer. I didn't ever think of him as anything but my blood brother." Harry stopped. A look of sadness clouded his face. Rose wasn't sure he'd continue until he spoke once again.

"My father and mother were getting along much better by then, and I was proud of Mom for treating Richard the same as she treated me. She'd accepted him and he grew to love her as if she was his own mother."

Rose squeezed Harry's warm hand affectionately once again. "My, that's quite a story. I can't picture my father living a double life like that. My mother would have killed him."

"Well, Father wasn't a bad man, just a weak man, as some of us are." Harry removed his hand from under Rose's. He drained the rest of the tea in his mug and sat back. "What about you dear? What was it like growing up for you?"

Rose spent an hour giving Harry sketchy details of her youth. She told him about her strict mother, her quiet father and wild brother. She skipped whole parts of her life, leaving out the secret she kept locked so tightly inside. She talked of the all-girls school, and then she spoke of the beloved aunt she'd lived with.

The time was late when Harry got up to return to his own apartment. "This was a wonderful day, Rose. I feel I know you so much more. Thank you for sharing your stories with me and allowing me to share mine." Harry reached over and kissed Rose gently on the lips before heading out the door.

While Rose crocheted that evening, rocking in her favorite chair, she reviewed the day and the stories she and Harry spoke of. What still puzzled her was his relationship with his sons, especially the young one, Tim. It wasn't her place to ask questions about them, but she wished she had some answers. Rose's chin dropped to her chest as sleep overtook her. She awoke at midnight to the shrill sound of the phone. Her heart pounded as she got up to answer it. It couldn't be good news. A ringing phone at this time was terrifying.

A frantic voice spoke quickly, words pouring out almost unintelligible.

"It's my father," she heard at last. "Rose, he's had a heart attack."

"Who is this?" Rose rubbed sleep from her eyes. Buttons looked up at her blinking his green cat eyes.

"It's Abby, Harry's daughter. My father just called and said he'd been having chest pains. The ambulance is there now, Rose. I'm on my way. I'm sorry to bother you and scare you like this, but would you please go over there and be with him until I can get there?"

"My goodness, poor Harry. Yes, Abby, I'll go right away."

Rose headed over to 5-C as fast as she could. Harry's door was ajar, the ambulance sat in front of his apartment, the lights flashing. Two stocky paramedics had Harry loaded onto a stretcher. An oxygen mask covered half his face, yet the blue eyes were open and clear. His coloring seemed a bit ashen, but otherwise, Harry didn't look much different from when Rose saw him earlier.

"Is he going to be okay?" Rose asked barely above a

whisper. Fear stole into her heart at the sight of this wonderful man, her new friend. The thought of losing him.

"Are you a relative?" The dark-haired paramedic asked.

"No, I'm just a good friend," Rose said. "His daughter phoned me a few minutes ago. She's on her way."

Just then, a car flew into a parking space near the front of the building. Two men got out and practically ran into the apartment. Rose recognized Sean and Tim, Harry's two sons.

"Is our father alright?" Sean asked, out of breath.

"We think so, sir," the other paramedic said. "We're taking him to Excela Health in Latrobe. That's the closest hospital. We'll get him there as soon as we can. His signs look pretty decent though. He's a strong man."

Sean blew out a long breath. His brother seemed visibly shaken. He went over to Harry and put his hand out to touch him. "Daddy," he said, "it's me, Timmy. I'm here for you. You're gonna be okay."

Harry gave a weak "thumbs up" to them, and the paramedics whisked him out the door.

"Let's go, Tim," Sean said. He turned to Rose. "Thank you so much for checking on him. Thank you for your kindness to my dad today."

As they all left the apartment, Sean locked the door, and said to his brother, "Do you think we should wait for Abby?"

Tim shook his head. "Let's try to follow the ambulance. It

may take her an hour to get here." He smiled weakly at Rose and then slipped into the passenger side of the car.

Rose walked the few steps to her apartment, watching the ambulance and car speed away. The younger son's almost frantic concern puzzled her. He seemed like a completely different person from the man she'd met earlier. There was something about him. . . For the first time in her life, she uttered a prayer.

"Please God, if you're there. Please take care of my friend, Harry, and Lord, bless his relationship with his family."

Chapter Ten

Abby watched her frail-looking father as he lay in the hospital bed. He'd been in the critical care unit for two days. Tubes and wires circled around him, a heart monitor blipping to the rhythm of Harry's heartbeats, yet he was smiling and doing his best to joke with the nurse who monitored his blood pressure.

"I guess you're the one making my blood pressure rise," he said to the young petite nurse as she wrote notes on a clipboard. Harry tried his best at initiating a wink. "They didn't make em' like you in my day." A small coughing fit ensued, and the nurse in question offered Harry a sip of water from the straw in his plastic glass.

"Now, Mr. McMillen, you must rest." The nurse rolled her eyes in Abby's direction, but a sweet smile remained on her face. "You're being transferred to a regular room today if everything keeps looking as good as it's been. You're one strong man." She patted his arm gently and put the glass on Harry's table.

"Do you think Dr. Cooper will be in this morning?" Abby asked. She watched her father's monitors and fretted about numbers and blips.

"He already made the rounds this morning," the nurse answered. "Your dad's doing well. It was a very mild heart attack, and all the numbers look great now. There was some question about blood work, nothing to be alarmed about. I'll make sure to check on it before he's transferred." She turned back to Harry. "I'll miss you, Mr. McMillen. It's been my distinct pleasure."

"Oh Daddy," Abby walked closer to her father's bed and stroked his graying hair with her hand. "You gave us all quite a scare. I'm so glad you're going to be fine. You've got to take it easy, okay?"

Harry turned his face away. Abby wondered if she'd hurt him with something she said. "Daddy, what's the matter?"

"I'm an old man," Harry began, still not looking at his daughter. "I've lived a good long life and had more than my share of blessings. I wonder sometimes why God chooses to keep me here."

"I can think of some reasons," Abby answered. "Your grandkids are one of them, and I think God has blessed you with a new dear friend in Rose."

Now Harry turned his face toward his daughter. He smiled, a tired smile, but reached for Abby's hand. "Yes, she is a fine lady and dear friend. No replacement for your mama, though. But I'm fortunate to know her." He paused, and then whispered, "Abby, I want to apologize, honey. I've hurt you children so much, haven't I?"

"Daddy, it's fine. We've been over this before. You're forgiven." Abby thought about her brother Timmy. Except for him. . . Yet Tim had driven with their brother Sean the night of their father's heart attack. He'd seemed worried sick over Daddy. I have to speak with him, Abby thought. I think it's time he and I have the talk that has been a long time coming.

"Daddy, I'll be back tonight when you're in a regular room, okay?" Abby picked her purse from the chair and slung it over her shoulder. After kissing her father, she left the room.

Abby rode the elevator to the floor that housed the snack bar. She pulled her cell phone from her purse and dialed Tim's number. She'd bought him a new phone when she found he had lost his. Abby knew Tim didn't have the money to purchase another. She'd spent most of her life bailing her younger brother out of jams, financially and otherwise. How she hoped he'd grow up soon.

Tim answered on the third ring. From the sound of his voice, Abby must have wakened him. "Hey Timmy, it's Ab. I need to talk to you."

"Ah, okay, sis, I'm uh, I'm just getting up to go on an interview later today."

Abby knew this was a lie. Though Tim needed a job desperately, he was unwilling to commit to anything. It wasn't that her brother was lazy, it was more like sadness, a depression he was unable to shake.

"Can I drive over to your place?" Abby asked. She sat at a small table in a corner of the cafeteria trying to keep her voice low. Doctors and nurses sat nearby and what appeared to be family groups at other tables. Abby wished she wasn't alone just then. She always had to be the strong one in their family. The one who cared too much.

"Uh, no, that's, uh, not a good idea right now," Tim answered. "Tell you what. I have to go over to Mom and Dad's house after my, uh, interview. Would you be able to meet me there?"

"Yes, that's fine. I'm with Dad now, but I can leave and be at their house in about an hour. Is that okay?"

"Yep, see you around two." Tim hung up.

Tim McMillen sat on the edge of the bed, running his finger over several days' growth of stubbly beard. How he wished it was the truth. He wished there was an interview today. But here he was in this crummy little apartment with Crystal. She lay on the other side of the bed, breathing deeply in slumber. Her job as cocktail waitress brought her home sometimes around four in the morning so he knew she'd probably sleep until three or so this afternoon. Tim shivered as he looked at the still form of his current girlfriend. Though she was a hard worker, her spending habits were becoming a bit much for this relationship. Tim's unemployment was due to run out in a few months, and the money Crystal brought in barely covered rent and utilities. Their credit card debt was stacking up.

Tim shuffled to the little bathroom down the hallway, kicking at piles of clothing. It shouldn't be this way, he thought. I'm better than this, aren't I?

A little later, seated in the grubby kitchen with flecks from a meal a few days ago crusted to the table, Tim held onto his cup of coffee. He reviewed recent events. The way he'd run when he thought something was really wrong with his father. Their relationship hadn't always been strained. There was a time, when he was a small child, that Harry had been Tim's hero. He'd wanted to be just like him when he grew up. Harry was the kind of father who played with his kids, made snowmen with them in the yard, patiently taught the boys how to throw a baseball and built that amazing wooden fort for them.

That was long ago. Tim couldn't help but picture the time he'd learned to hate his father. The times he'd seen him flirting with different women from the church congregation. No, there were too many conflicting feelings Tim couldn't shake when he thought about his father. Then the final straw. Carol Heckert, the church secretary. He could barely think the name. Carol, a nice woman who organized all the plays in the church and taught Sunday school too. Yeah, Tim thought, Carol organized some plays all right especially the one with his dad. At first Tim blamed her, and then as time went on, Tim saw his father for the weak-willed man he was. All the while his mother knew nothing, nor suspected a thing. When Tim had gone to his siblings about what he'd seen, they both dismissed him as having an outrageous imagination, a scandalous mind. It wasn't until Sean saw for himself when he returned from college one semester that his brother and sister truly knew what their father was doing.

Tim was helping sweep up discarded pamphlets and Styrofoam coffee cups from around the seats in the auditorium after the Christmas play. He liked this time in the church, the quiet after hours when all the people were gone. It was a time to reflect, to pretend that someday, he, too, would be pastor of this church and have a loving congregation like his father did. He stepped onto the stage for a moment, standing behind the podium looking out at the faces he knew he'd see someday. People with rapturous attention, hanging on his every Godly word.

The sound of giggling brought ten-year-old Tim out of his reverie. It was coming from behind the stage, the dressing room perhaps. Tim crept around back and as he neared the door of the room, he heard hushed voices. He recognized Mrs. Heckert's voice, the director of the plays, and could swear the other was his father's.

Tim heard breathless whispers and words of love pass between the two people as he eavesdropped outside the door.

He peered around the door, careful not to make a sound. What he'd seen had floored him then, as he spotted his father and Mrs. Heckert locked in each other's arms. It sickened him; he couldn't fathom what he was seeing. True, he'd seen his father before flirting shamelessly with others, but this was too much for his young mind.

Tim heard his brother's voice then, calling for him. Sean was home for Christmas break from college and had come to pick Timmy up. He ran around to the front of the stage as Sean was making his way down the aisle. He put a finger to his lips and pointed back at the stage. When his brother asked what was going on, Tim had gotten ill. Cold and clammy, he'd passed out for a few seconds. Sean must have heard the voices himself, because after Tim came to, the look on his brother's face spoke volumes.

Tim opened the crumpled newspaper before him as the memories faded into precious oblivion. Perhaps there would be a job for him, something to pass the time where he could make a few bucks. This endless waiting game couldn't go on forever. When he thought about it, though, he wondered just what he was waiting for. Dad to die? Was that it? Dad to beg his forgiveness? Hadn't he already done that a few years ago? No, it was Dad, for Dad to know Tim, to really see him when he looked at him. Not this stupid "Richard" thing that his father had been calling him.

Tim didn't understand dementia. He wasn't patient enough to learn the facts about it and how it might rob his father of precious memories, even perhaps losing sight of who his family was. All Tim saw was a self-centered man who purposely chose not to acknowledge his youngest son because, if it wasn't for Tim, Harry's beloved wife Julie might still be alive. Tim felt in his heart that his dad blamed him for Mom's death. That by telling her Harry's secrets, she'd died of a broken heart.

Tim threw the newspaper down and ran a hand through his unwashed hair. Why he'd chosen to tell his mother in her late sixties about Dad's dalliances was beyond him. Maybe he was trying to hurt Harry by doing so. But it had backfired and Mom never believed her youngest son. Not during the screaming battle that went on and on that night, nor in the days leading up to her stroke.

Tim drained the last of the bitter coffee in his cup, guilt cloaking him like a suffocating blanket. Perhaps his brother and sister were right. Maybe it was he who needed to change and end this nonsense once and for all. Make up to the old man, wish him well, and get on with his life. Tim stood, looking out the small window into the alley below and uttered a short prayer: *God, please help me.*

Chapter Eleven

*R*ose laid an ace upon Harry's table in the hospital room he shared with another gentleman. "Rummy," she said and giggled.

"Now Rose, that's not fair," Harry said, sweeping the playing cards to the side. "I think you're cheating." He winked at her, those blue sparkling eyes, clear as a summer's day. "Ed, what do you think?" Harry asked the older man in the second bed.

"I think I need a good woman like Rosie," he quipped, and they all broke into laughter.

"You men are impossible," Rose said. "I'm an old goat. You need the young pretty nurses that I keep seeing walking up and down the hallway." Rose shuffled the deck of cards again.

"I think you're prettier than any of them," Ed Keller said. "As a matter of fact when my wife gets here later, we'll ask her too." He laughed again, a joyous sound in the bland setting of a hospital room.

As Rose dealt the cards, she watched Harry's face scrunch, the way it looked when he was trying to think of something challenging.

"It was good seeing my brother," Harry said quietly, almost to himself.

Rose gulped. What was Harry saying? From what he'd told her, Richard had passed on a few years back. She laid her hand on top of Harry's arm.

"Harry, whatever you're talking about, it couldn't have been Richard . ." Rose trailed off. Harry's eyes blazed in anger.

"I know my own darn brother when I see him," he said, pushing the cards away once again. "I don't want to play anymore." He crossed his arms in front of himself.

Just then, Abby and the children strolled into the room. The twins each carried a large, toy stuffed animal in their hands, while the baby broke into the sweetest grin at seeing her grandpa. Rose watched as Harry composed himself after becoming so mean with her. His grandkids no doubt were the joy of his life.

"Hey, little Abby," he said, holding his arms out for the baby. Rose watched Abby's face as she caught her father mistaking the baby's name once again, but quickly put a finger to her lips and shook her head silently. Harry's memory seemed bad tonight.

"We dropped by to see you, Daddy, and also to get Rose

back to her place later." Abby deposited the baby in her father's arms while Nicholas wriggled onto the bed beside Harry, and Gavin stayed shyly at his mother's side.

"I spent the afternoon with Timmy," Abby said, and Rose noticed she watched her father's face carefully as she said this.

Harry appeared as if he hadn't heard a thing. He bounced Allison gently while she chortled in his arms.

"Just let me know when you're ready to leave, honey," Rose said, trying to change the subject. She stood from the chair and straightened her back. "I had dinner with Harry tonight already, and it's been a pretty long day."

"We won't stay too long." Abby looked at her father once again. "Daddy, can I ask you something?" Harry stopped bouncing the baby for a minute and looked at his daughter.

"Why do you get so quiet when I mention Tim? Are you angry with him?"

But Harry no longer looked at his daughter. His attention had gone back to the baby. He tickled her and she giggled, a most beautiful sound.

Abby shrugged her shoulders, appearing to give up on this particular conversation. She made small talk about the children and her husband. She told Harry he'd be leaving the hospital the next day. Rose watched Abby's face. Though usually calm, she appeared to be carrying an extra burden.

~*~

Before Abby left that night, she walked into the hall outside his room. She wanted to speak to someone. Her father seemed exceptionally confused today. A nurse she'd seen before wheeled a cart of medicines a few doorways down. Abby walked over to her.

"Hi, I'm Harry McMillen's daughter, Abby." The careworn nurse looked up from her cart and her face softened immediately.

"What's the matter, honey?" The nurse asked. "You look like you have the weight of the world on your shoulders."

"That bad, huh?" Abby asked, brushing a stray lock of hair from the ponytail she'd put it in earlier. "It's just that, well, my father really seems more confused than before. He's scaring me a little. He's already been showing signs of forgetfulness, but I wondered if something happened or if he was given some type of medication."

"Maybe this will help," the nurse said, giving Abby her full attention. "Sometimes when people who already have Alzheimer's or some type of dementia are placed into stressful situations, such as a hospital, their condition may appear to become aggravated a bit. Symptoms often increase while they're here, but when they return home, they go back to normal." She touched Abby's arm as she spoke.

"I'll check on him when you leave and make sure he's doing well. He's scheduled for discharge tomorrow. He's a good guy. And really lucky to have a daughter who cares as much as you do."

Abby thanked the nurse and breathed a small sigh of relief. Though her conversation with Tim still hurt her terribly, she calmed herself and walked back into the room.

Around seven thirty, Abby gathered the children and Rose and bid her dad goodnight. She would try to get to Huntington after the medical van picked Harry up in the morning to return him to his apartment.

Abby drove in silence for a while, her thoughts jumbled, her heart saddened. She'd spent several hours with Tim, letting him absolve himself of the burden he carried. She'd never known about what happened with Mom. Never known that Tim had been so callous and hurtful. She'd always thought the reason he and their father didn't speak was because of the affair. That Tim was the one who didn't forgive. But now she had reason to think her father harbored bitter anger toward her brother. He really did blame him for Mom's stroke and subsequent death. Oh, this was all too much.

Abby turned the CD player on, Barry Manilow crooned softly into the van.

"I like this music," Rose said, relaxing into the passenger seat. "Thank you for taking me home, dear. It's been quite a long day. When I've had to travel by senior bus, and all the stops they have to make, it wears me out."

Abby glanced in the rearview mirror. All the children were asleep. *Do I open up to this woman? Just how do I know if I might not ruin her relationship with Daddy? She's so kind, so good. Am I wrong for needing someone to talk to?*

"Rose," Abby said, clearing her throat, taking a swig of water from the plastic bottle in the console between them. "I need to come clean about a few things. I wonder if you'd mind if I talk with you. It's been so long, you see, since I've had a mother to talk to. I miss her so much. And though my Tom is a wonderful man, there's just something about talking with another woman."

"I'd be honored if you'd open up to me, Abby. Only if you want to though."

For the remainder of the drive, Abby spoke about her parents. She told Rose about the good and bad of being a child of a preacher. How sometimes she blamed God for taking her father from them for the long hours he put into his parish, and felt so guilty afterward for having such thoughts. She spoke of her saintly mother, a quiet, compassionate soul, who had more patience than anyone she'd ever known.

Abby began to cry when she talked about her father's indiscretion but she was powerless to stop. It all came flooding out of her. Even what Tim had told her today about being the cause of their mother's death.

When she was done, she swiped at the tears. "You must hate me," Abby said. "And I'm afraid you must really hate my father now. I meant no harm, Rose. I just had this bottled up for so long."

Rose laid a hand on Abby's arm. The CD player slid to the next disc, and Michael Crawford sang out from the Phantom of the Opera. "Abby, I am not upset with you at all. Nor do I hate anyone. You see, I have my own past. I have heartache so bad I've not shaken it from the time I was a young girl. My own daughter doesn't speak to me. She blames me for her problems; she doesn't even care for me at all." Now it was Rose's turn to cry. She pulled several Kleenex from the bottom of her purse.

"I lost a baby when I was very young. And it was so traumatizing for me, well, I had a mental breakdown over it later in life. When Toni, that's my daughter, was a young girl, I was consumed with worry for her. What if I lost her? What if she, too, died like the baby? It was too much for me. I wanted to die sometimes. You see, we all have our stories, don't we?"

Abby turned into the parking space in front of Rose's apartment. Shutting off the engine, she turned to Rose. "You are one of the most beautiful people I've ever met, Rose. I think you're awfully brave to tell me your story. Thank you. This was a very difficult day for me. It really helped sharing with you."

"You can talk to me anytime," Rose said. "Perhaps we can have a crocheting lesson again soon. I'd really like that."

"Do you need help getting to your place?"

"No, I'll be fine. Goodnight, Abby." Rose opened the door of the minivan and climbed carefully out. Waving from her little porch stoop, she sighed as she watched Abby drive off into the night.

Chapter Twelve

*T*oni Warner paced the floor of her office. She'd been up since three a.m. Looking at herself in the mirror behind her desk, she touched the dark circles under each eye, hating the way this made her feel. Nothing was right. It had been a week since Ben had stayed with her. True, he'd asked to come by almost every night. But she got even less sleep when he was around. She kicked the empty waste can with the toe of her high-heeled shoe, sending it sprawling across the floor.

Toni picked her cell phone up for at least the fourth time. She glanced at the time, ten thirty. Too early for a drink. What should she do? Her mother's face came strongly into her mind once again. That pretty, but haunted face. *What kind of monster am I? It's been months now since we've spoken. What must she think of me?* This never bothered Toni before. Was she growing a heart perhaps?

Without a second thought, Toni pressed the button that would phone her mother. The ringing went on for what felt like eternity when her mother finally picked up.

"Hello?"

Toni shut her eyes. Memories came flooding back. Memories of that empty house, the fear she'd felt as a small girl. The way kids made fun of her when they learned her mother was in a loony bin.

"Hi, Mama."

"Toni? Oh my goodness. Are you alright?" That panicked sound in her mother's voice, that almost hysterical edge to it.

"Yes, of course, I'm fine," Toni snapped. *Hold on, be kinder. . . Lose the attitude.*

"H-how have you been?" Toni closed her eyes, breathing deeply in through the nose out through the mouth.

"I'm well honey. Would you. . ." she hesitated for a moment. "Would you like to come by for dinner sometime soon?"

"Yes, okay," Toni said. "Perhaps this weekend, alright? I have a gentleman friend I'd like you to meet, if, uh, if that's good for you?"

"Oh, yes, I'd love that."

Toni could hear the smile in her mother's voice, the relief. "Let's say this Sunday then at two? And I have a gentleman friend I'd like you to meet as well."

Toni's mouth dropped open. A gentleman? Her mother? "Y- yes, Mama, okay. That will be fine. See you then." She pressed the button on her phone, disconnecting the call.

Picking up her car keys, she headed out the door. "Jodi, hold all my calls this afternoon would you? I need the afternoon off."

~*~

Rose hugged herself when she hung up the phone. Her daughter called. She didn't hate her after all. In her mind, Rose already mentally began preparing the meal she'd make for Sunday. So Toni had a young man? Perhaps that softened her. She was too independent, too alone, and Rose feared she'd never grow close to anyone, never know what true love was all about.

Rose walked over to her portrait, the picture of the young girl on the wicker chair. Nobody knew this was she. Only one person and that was her own true love, Skip. He'd painted it when they hadn't been able to see one another again. He'd tried to bring it over to her that day, to show her how he captured her loveliness, her innocence, but her father made him leave, never to return.

What Father hadn't counted on though was Skip's good friend who'd brought it to her one sunny afternoon. He'd introduced himself as Hunter, and after chatting with Rose as she strolled the grounds outside her massive home, had asked her to wait while he retrieved something in his vehicle. Hunter had come back with the large parcel under his arm, wrapped in brown paper. Rose could still smell the fresh paint even now.

When she tore the paper off and saw the portrait of herself, she'd burst into tears. Skip's friend had held her then, stroking her hair tenderly, telling her just how much Skip really loved her, and how much it meant to him to paint this picture. Rose said goodbye after her mother had come out onto the porch and, in a demanding voice, ordered Hunter away. Mother wanted to destroy the painting, but Father begged her to let their daughter keep it. After all, it was a beautiful likeness of Rose. The quality of the portrait was exquisite.

Rose traced the signature with her finger. Skip Parkinson. Scrawled so messily nobody else had ever been able to read it. But Rose knew. She could imagine him signing it, knowing he'd never see his darling again, but hoping against all hope, she'd at least have this gift to treasure.

Rose brought herself back to the present. Walking into her kitchen, she began opening cupboards, making mental notes of some items she'd need for the dinner. She chuckled to herself thinking how much she probably floored poor Toni when she mentioned a gentleman friend too. Harry had been home about three days now, and he looked better than ever. It was his memory that was beginning to scare them all. Abby spoke a little about it the night she and Rose drove home from the hospital.

Rose hadn't for one minute been upset over all the stories Abby shared that evening. Harry had an affair in his marriage.

It wasn't in Rose's power to condemn him, or judge him critically. She certainly made a mess of her own young life. If anything, she felt she understood him even more. A good man, yet flawed, and now she knew she was in love with him. She'd been fortunate to find love in the twilight years. Humming a tune from Phantom of the Opera, Rose pulled cans of tomato sauce from the cabinet.

Chapter Thirteen

*H*arry sat on Rose's couch, his best crisp blue cotton shirt buttoned to the top, a black tie completing his elegant look. Rose felt her heart flutter. At his age, he was still a strikingly handsome man. Rose glanced in the mirror near her front door, her stomach awash with nervous butterflies as her daughter was due any moment.

"How do I look?" she asked Harry for at least the fifth time.

"You're one of the most beautiful women I've ever seen." Blue eyes sparkled. "Come here."

Harry pulled Rose onto his lap, holding her gently, almost rocking her like a small child. "You smell wonderful too, honey," he said. "Don't be scared. Would you like me to pray for you?"

Rose nodded her head. Though she still wasn't completely comfortable with prayer, the way Harry said things gave her strength and made her whole. He spoke a small personal prayer as he held her.

A knock at the door sounded, and Rose jumped up. Smoothing her hands over her silky floral dress, she walked calmly to the door.

Toni and a young, dark haired man stood on her stoop. The young man broke into the biggest smile, extending his hand with a bouquet of yellow roses.

"Why, thank you. Please come in." Rose looked at her daughter. Too skinny and pale, but she still was pretty. Toni appeared nervous, and she held onto the man's hand as if she might collapse.

"Mama, this is Ben. Ben Stevens. This is my mother, Ben."

Rose put out her hand for a greeting, but felt herself enveloped into a warm embrace by the young man.

"My pleasure, Rose," he said. "My, you're every bit as pretty as Toni said."

Rose walked ahead of them to the couch where Harry sat. "This is my friend, Harry." Ben shook Harry's hand as he rose, and Toni put out a slender hand.

"Please, sit everyone." Rose said. "I have some stuffed mushrooms, and Harry, would you please open the bottle of wine?"

"Oh, let me," Ben said. He reached for the bottle of Riesling chilling on the sideboard and uncorked it in one practiced stroke. Pouring a little for each of them into the crystal goblets sitting nearby, Ben toasted to a wonderful afternoon.

Rose's stuffed shells were the hit of the day. Her Aunt Hilda had taught her culinary skills among other things during her brief time with her. Rose talked about the dear woman who'd been like a sister to her.

"Oh, yes, Ben," Rose said. "My aunt was once a cook for some very famous people; the Kaufmann's and even the Aster's. She taught me everything about preparing elegant foods from scratch." Rose picked her glass of wine up and after taking a small sip, she began speaking again.

"Hilda never married, you see. She was what was known as an old spinster. But nobody knew her like I did. She had a very humorous side, a very fun, adventurous side. Though she taught me crocheting and homemaking, we sometimes went to comedy clubs and plays. That's how I met my Alex."

Rose watched as Toni appeared more relaxed. *This is a side of me she's never seen before*, Rose thought. *And she's never heard the story of how me and her father met.*

"Alex was in one of the plays we watched one evening. It was Hamlet, and he was only an extra in the background. I'd caught his eye though, as Hilda and I had front row seats, and he told me later that he hadn't been able to concentrate after seeing me." Rose felt her face grow hot, whether from the wine or reliving this very personal memory, she wasn't sure.

"That's wonderful, Mama." Toni said. "What a charming story about Daddy." She drained her own glass of wine and got up to clear plates from the table.

"Let me help," Rose said. "You boys head on into the living room. Perhaps you can find a good movie on TV."

When they were alone in the kitchen, Toni turned to her mother. "Can you forgive me?" she asked. "I've been very selfish. I'm so sorry." She put her head down.

Rose picked up her daughter's chin and looked her frankly in the eyes. "You and I aren't the same people we once were. There's nothing to forgive, Toni. Let's move on with our lives and be happy for one another. There's no time like the present for us to begin again."

Rose pulled her daughter into a warm hug as Toni's tears began to fall. She patted Toni's silky hair, smoothing it, whispering soothing words.

"I'll do better, Mama," Toni said. "I- I promise." She hugged her mother back this time.

~*~

A little later, seated in the living room with cups of coffee and pieces of warm blackberry pie, the talk was lighthearted and simple. Rose glowed, knowing those she loved best in the world were right there in the room with her.

"This is wonderful," Toni said, admiring the multi-color

afghan gracing the arm of the couch. "You're going to have to teach me sometime. I never cared about this when I was younger."

"Oh, I'd love that," Rose said taking a bite of pie. She saw Harry rise from his seat, straighten his back and walk over to her wall of paintings.

He scratched his head as he stood before the portrait of Rose. "Rose," he asked. "Is this you by any chance?" His face scrunched in the way it did when he either had a memory lapse or was thinking very hard of something.

"Why, yes, it is," Rose answered. "I was seventeen in that picture, and the person who painted it did it from memory. I wasn't sitting for him you see. It's very special, that one."

Harry traced the scrawled signature in the corner. "I know this picture," he said.

"Well, of course you do," Rose said. "You've seen it here before." Yet she watched as Harry appeared deep in thought.

"No, that's not it," he said. "I've seen this or one just like it."

As Ben began telling stories about his family, Harry walked away from the portrait, scratching his head. Mumbling to himself under his breath, he told Rose he had to leave.

"Aren't you feeling well?" she asked.

"Oh, I'm fine, just fine. A little tired is all. So nice to have met you two," Harry said as he picked up his light sport jacket.

"I'll talk to you tomorrow, Rose." He pecked her briefly on the cheek before leaving.

Rose sat back with her daughter and Ben, a little puzzled over Harry's behavior, but reveling in the warm glow of love and family.

When Toni and Ben left near nine p.m., Rose made her way into her bedroom, and began undressing for the night. She laid her dress carefully over the armchair in the room while Buttons sidled up to her. The Thumbelina doll which had been such a big part of her world, sat swaddled in a small blanket on the chair. When she climbed into bed, Rose realized something. She hadn't needed her doll around her for days.

Chapter Fourteen

"*A*re you sure, Daddy?" Abby asked on the phone. "What makes you so certain?"

"I know my brother's work, even his scribbled signature. Richard painted the portrait on Rose's wall."

Abby rolled her eyes. Dad was spouting nonsense again. His obsession with his brother lately was getting old. Timmy must resemble their uncle at that age or something. But this painting now, it was just weird.

"Daddy, did your brother sell his work? Perhaps that's how Rose came by this picture. You said her husband bought her most of the artwork on her walls, right?"

"Richard never sold his artwork. He usually did it for people he cared about. I always told him he should have done something with it. He was that good."

"Well, I'll ask Rose where she got it sometime, Daddy. For now, how have you been feeling?"

As Harry spoke, Abby's mind wandered. Perhaps she

should get her father tested again. His memory appeared to be heading downhill faster these days. He didn't want to take medication for the lapses, but perhaps there was something he could do that would stave off the inevitable.

"Daddy, would you object to seeing Dr. Shoat again?" Abby, who was sitting in her recliner sideways, bolted straight up with her dad's answer.

"I'm not seeing that quack ever again, young lady. Don't you ever mention that to me, you understand? My mind's perfectly fine. Maybe you're the one who needs to see him."

Abby's heart sank. Never before had her father talked to her this way. So angry, so full of spiteful sarcasm. She knew this could be another symptom of Alzheimer's type dementia. Someone not acting like themselves. Mean and hateful words spewing from them as the disease began ravaging their brains.

"I'm sorry," she said, then changed the subject. "Did you have a nice dinner with Rose and her daughter? Tell me all about it."

While her dad talked, Abby paced the floor. She heard Allison crying and excused herself from the rest of the conversation. Later when Tom arrived home from work, she voiced her concern to him.

"Ab, just like your father needs to start walking with a cane, he also has to begin taking some type of medicine." Tom lay on the living room floor, his children spread around him as he read from their favorite book, *Green Eggs and Ham*. "Maybe our little friend Rose can work her magic with him. After all, they really are quite the item, aren't they?"

Abby joined her family on the plush carpet. She scooped Allison onto her lap, rubbing noses with her and giving butterfly kisses with her eyelashes.

"I think I'll call Rose and see about another crocheting session with her. Then I can grill her a bit about Dad." Abby let a long breath out and closed her eyes. How much longer did they have until their father really started losing precious memories? Or was his case something entirely different? No, she would see if Rose would gently bring up the subject with her dad.

~*~

"Well, how do you like it?" Abby pulled the beginnings of the lap afghan she'd been working on out of the fabric bag she brought to Rose's place.

Rose turned it this way and that, her bent fingers playing over the soft yarn, a slight smile breaking out onto her face.

"Well, dear, it's pretty good, but it looks like you missed counting here. See?" Rose laid the blanket across Abby's lap and stretched it out. It appeared like a distorted rectangle. The edges were longer on some rows, shorter on others.

Abby laughed, pushing her long hair out of her face. "I guess I do need more lessons then, huh?"

As Rose demonstrated the simple triple stitch once again, Abby's eyes wandered to the wall of paintings.

"Rose, you do have some lovely artwork."

Still bent over her work, Rose mumbled, "Uh hum."

"My father was quite impressed last week with the one of the young girl and the cat. It's you, he said?"

"Why, yes, it is." Rose said in a rather halting voice.

"May I ask who painted it?"

Rose stopped what she was doing. The urge to grab her Thumbelina doll rose in her. Thoughts of Skip, thoughts of the lost baby, all came flooding back.

She looked at Abby, her eyes filling with tears.

"I'm so sorry," Abby said, reaching for tissues atop the coffee table. "It must be very personal to you. I- I shouldn't have pried."

"Nonsense," Rose said, dabbing at her eyes. Thoughts of the baby doll vanished. Rose felt braver, calmer. Resolve rose up in her as she faced Abby.

"I have a story to tell you," she said, a faraway look in her eyes. Rose laid the yarn, hook and blanket off to the side.

"I was seventeen when that was painted. The young man who did it was my beau. He was a man my family didn't approve of. His name was Skip, and we were in love.

"It wasn't long before we were. . .intimate with one another. It was the nineteen fifties, and good young girls didn't do that sort of thing, you see. But Skip held my heart like no other, and it wasn't something I felt dirty about. We'd talked of marriage, of being together for the rest of our lives.

"Well, I'd begun feeling ill, throwing up and all. I passed out one day after a terrible argument with my mother, and woke up in a hospital room to find I was pregnant with Skip's child." Rose stopped. Sadness cloaked her, overwhelming her. She sighed, a deep, long sigh.

"The unthinkable happened. My mother forced me into an abortion. I. . . I haven't spoken of this to anyone in many, many years. I'm not sure why I felt so strongly to tell you this." Tears flowed freely now, unbidden, cleansing.

"Please continue," Abby said, moving closer to Rose, laying her hand on her arm. "If you want to, that is. I'd love to hear about the painting."

"About a week or two after that shameful surgery, I heard voices outside my window. I'd been locked up in my room recuperating and hadn't been out for any reason. I walked over and peered outside to see Skip talking with my father. You see, Skip had painted that lovely portrait and he wanted to bring it as a peace offering to my family, but mostly for me to cherish. Father sent him away never to return, and I watched the man I'd wanted to marry, drive away after he threw a package into the back of his truck.

"It wasn't until a few weeks later, when Skip's good

friend, Hunter, found me outside one day, that the picture was given to me. I knew I'd never be allowed to see Skip, to thank him, or talk to him about all that happened. But his friend was so kind, and relayed our message to one another. My parents let me keep the painting. It's all I have of him now."

"Oh, Rose," Abby reached over to hold the woman tightly. "What a brave, young girl you must have been. What a sad, sad story."

"I feel better for telling you," Rose said. "In some ways, hiding it has been much harder on me." She picked the crocheting back up.

Abby laughed. "My father seemed to think his late brother Richard painted it. I'm worried about him. He obsesses over Richard. Calls Timmy that name all the time. I think his mind is slipping away faster, Rose." Abby got up and walked over to the painting.

"I tried talking with my father about seeing Dr. Shoat who's a great specialist in Alzheimer's and dementia. I was hoping Daddy would perhaps agree to take medication. I've heard it helps certain people."

Rose, who had been listening carefully, felt herself stop breathing for a moment. Just then, she realized what had bothered her so much about Abby's younger brother Tim. Just how much he resembled Skip the last time she'd seen him.

"So would you mind speaking to him?" Abby finished.

"Uh, yes, of course, dear. I'll talk with him. You can count on it." Rose patted the couch next to her. "Now let's continue, shall we?"

Chapter Fifteen

As summer wore on, the oppressive heat blanketed the town. However, It didn't stop a few of the residents of Huntington from heading to one of their annual outings. They rode the senior van to the picturesque downtown area of Ligonier to spend the day.

On one of the streets before the town diamond, Rose clapped her hands to her mouth. "Harry, would you look at that building? It was closed up for years. It looks like someone must have renovated it." Before them stood a massive Victorian-type home. Its sprawling grounds neatly kept and front porch inviting with cozy furniture. The sign before it read: Thisteldown at Seger House. Rose noticed it was now an inn.

"Someone really must have loved that old building. It's gorgeous," she said, while taking Harry's arm. "Can you imagine the stories it could tell?" Rose stood admiring the workmanship of the structure, her mind filled with images of romance. "I'd like to stay there someday."

Harry and Rose walked past many of the quaint, charming shops. Some of the shopkeepers had small tables in front of their stores with their wares lovingly displayed. Colorful pottery items sat before The Pottery Barn. Soft, wooly yarns in front of Bo-Peep's. Handmade, decorative greeting cards and even used books, their covers a bit tattered, in front of the local library. When Harry passed the Equine Chic shop, he stopped. Laying his hands against the glass, Rose watched as his face glowed with an expression of almost boyish charm. "Rose, would you look in there." Harry's finger pointed and Rose's eyes lit upon the item which seemed to bring him such joy. "My Dad used to have those." Through the window Rose saw a pair of well-worn riding boots their supple brown leather intact and horse blanket with small pictures of quarter horses prancing.

"You never told me your father was a horse man," Rose said. "You want to head inside and look?"

Harry sighed and shook his head. "No, it was a long time ago. Long before me and my brother were born. Dad kept his boots and blanket in pristine condition like he was saving it for something special. No, let's head over to the crowd and see what's going on."

The gazebo on the town diamond looked stunning with streamers, colorful banners, and white roses intertwined throughout. Mounds of well-tended flowers, marigolds, impatiens, and geraniums bordered the area. There wasn't a cloud in the deep blue sky. A young couple was about to wed there.

Rose stood among the crowd of onlookers as wedding music piped forth from speakers set up near the municipal building. The bride wore a flowing, sleeveless satin dress, and her groom and his men wore white tuxedos. Rose felt such happiness watching the young couple as the bride's father kissed her and placed her hand atop the groom's. Harry stood next to her, his hand at the small of her back. He whispered to Rose and said something that just about stole her breath.

"I wish that was me and you, honey. I wish we were that young and about to start a new life together." He kissed the top of Rose's head. She snuggled closer to him, though sweat trickled down her back in the hot sunshine of the day.

"Would you like to walk a little now?" Harry asked, gently pulling Rose away from the ceremony. "I promised you an ice cream cone."

They walked hand in hand, Rose admiring the old-world shops, stopping from time to time to admire some fancy or treat in different storefronts. As they stood before Second Chapter Books, a small bookstore, Rose motioned to Harry that she'd like to go inside.

Now it was Rose's turn to smile. Rows of books and gift

items filled every nook of the large room with another smaller room through a walkway. The owner, a sweet lady with a smile like sunshine, seemed to enjoy Rose's expression.

"You have quite an assortment in here," Rose remarked.

"Oh yes, we're very fortunate to have such great people donating their gently used copies of well-loved books. I can tell by the expression on your face, you must be a book lover."

"Oh, when I was a lot younger," Rose said. "I used to be able to finish a novel in a few days. Now crocheting takes up all my time."

"Well, enjoy browsing," the woman said, and busied herself with paperwork on the counter before her.

Rose looked through shelves of old titles and new, her fingers lingering a bit on some of the classics when Harry announced he had to use the restroom. Rose turned to the owner.

"Do you have a bathroom for patrons?" She held a copy of Gone With The Wind in her hands.

The owner of the store said she didn't, but the municipal building up the block had one for the public to use.

"I'll walk with you," Rose said, putting the book down.

"Are you sure, dear?" Harry asked. "If you'd just point me in the right direction, I'll meet you back here."

Rose glanced around the shop wistfully. "No, I better come with you. We can return later." She waved goodbye to the owner of the store as they headed out.

"I'd like to pick up some of that amazing homemade candy for Toni in here when you're through." Rose spotted the sign for the rest area while they passed Scamp's Tofee shop. She glanced at the mouthwatering assortment of light and dark chocolates gracing the window area.

Harry looked at his watch. "It's almost three, so we have another two hours before our van leaves. We'll get you whatever you want, my queen."

Rose walked with Harry through the throng of people, and left him at the front of the men's room. "I'll be sitting right over there on those benches." Rose pointed to several metal benches nearby.

While she sat, Rose fanned herself with a small map she'd picked up in town at a local realtor's office. The day felt hotter if it was possible. Time for something cold to drink. Maybe The Creamery, the ice cream shop, had a soft drink fountain.

Time passed and Rose stood, searching the faces of the people milling nearby for signs of Harry. She glanced up at the clock on the side of the building. Three twenty. My goodness, he's been in there a while.

Rose got up to stand near the entrance of the men's room. The crowd thinned a bit, and she asked another older gentleman, a bit embarrassed, if he'd check to see if someone fitting Harry's description was in there. A cold knob of fear attached itself to her stomach. What if he'd passed out?

The elderly man walked out a few minutes later. No, he'd not seen anybody else. He even checked for feet under the stalls, there wasn't another soul inside.

Panic settled full bloom in Rose. She looked around frantically. The wedding ceremony was over, and many people were gone. She noticed a few familiar faces of other residents from Huntington and made her way over to them.

"Have any of you seen Harry McMillen, the gentleman I came here with?" They shook their heads. "How about our supervisor, Lilly? I must find her and tell her what happened." Nobody had seen their supervisor of activities either.

Several of the men volunteered to help locate Harry. They broke off to look in the different shops, inquiring over and over if any of the people inside had seen Harry. It was no good. There wasn't one person who had.

At four thirty, Rose sat at one of the wooden benches near the gazebo. It was quiet now in town, the streamers and confetti from the wedding lay forlorn upon the ground, discarded, as several young people began sweeping up. Rose put her head in her hands and began to cry. What had begun as a lovely day turned into a tragedy. Her poor Harry. It frightened her to think where he may have wandered to. The older couple who tried helping her earlier had gone to find the police station. They told Rose to wait in case Harry came back.

Lilly Chalmers, the supervisor of activities from Huntington, ran over to Rose. "Whatever is wrong dear? The lady that runs the yarn shop told me you were looking for me."

"Harry McMillen is missing," Rose cried. "Several of us have been looking everywhere."

"Rose, my goodness. Let's get some help." As Rose explained to Lilly about Harry using the men's bathroom, a voice nearby screamed, "We found him!"

Rose looked up to see a bedraggled Harry being supported by two of the other residents. His polo shirt and khaki pants were rumpled and smeared with dirt, and his eyes. Rose ran up to Harry, throwing her arms around his neck. Harry appeared as if he almost didn't see her, as if he looked right through her. A blank expression was on his face, and this frightened Rose most of all.

"What happened?" Rose asked the kind male resident, the one who'd searched so frantically earlier.

"He was wandering the residential section of town. He said he felt a bit confused when he stepped out of the restroom and couldn't find a familiar face."

"Oh Harry, my poor Harry," Rose crooned over and over while she smoothed his silver hair, holding him as if she'd never let him go.

Just then he stirred a bit, clarity coming back into his eyes. "R-rose?"

"Yes, darling, I'm here. You're okay now."

"Oh, I'm such a fool. When I couldn't find you, I started looking, and. . ."

"Never you mind now. You're safe. Let's go board the van. We can talk at my apartment later."

~*~

Nancy Blackwell, a nurse from Huntington, squeezed the blood pressure cuff around the upper part of Harry's right arm. A thermometer dangled from the corner of his mouth while she finished the reading of his blood pressure. "One twenty over fifty-six," she announced. "Temperature ninety eight point six. I think you'll survive." She patted Harry's leg, her unsmiling, serious demeanor not a shock to Rose. Nancy was kind and she was thorough, yet she was never one to make jokes or take her job lightly.

"So he looks okay, Nancy?" Rose asked a slight quiver to her voice. She'd been shaken up quite badly today and couldn't rid herself of the feeling of impending doom.

"He's fine. He should follow up with his family physician, perhaps this week." Nancy began putting the stethoscope and blood pressure cuff away in her leather case. Snapping it shut, she turned to Harry. "You're a lucky man. You have a good lady here who cares about you." Turning to Rose, "Is there anything else you two need right now?" That kindness in her, Rose thought.

"No, we're fine. I'll see that Harry has something to eat with his nightly pills. Thanks so much, Nancy." Rose walked the nurse to the door, seeing her out before heading to the kitchen to heat up leftover chicken soup.

When they were seated a little later at her kitchen table, Rose decided it was time to be direct with Harry. It wasn't doing him any good, this tiptoeing around his forgetfulness. They had to confront it.

"Harry, I'm concerned for you," Rose began. She put her spoon down, waiting for Harry as he tilted the soup bowl toward his mouth, spilling some of the contents down the front of his shirt.

The feeling Rose had earlier watching the young couple marrying was replaced by the truth. They were old now. There was no mistaking the signs. The sloppiness, the memory lapses, health issues, all of it, the total package wrapped up in a neat bow. Was this the gift of old age?

Harry put his bowl down upon the table, flecks of noodles clinging to the front of his shirt. Rose picked up a napkin and dabbed at them.

"I want you to start using a cane, first of all," she said. "I've seen how unsteady you are on your feet. I don't want you to fracture your ribs or any other part of you, okay?" Rose's tone commanded attention. She'd meant it to sound harsh. Harry nodded.

"Now, another thing. I want you to see the doctor Abby recommended about your memory." She saw Harry was about to protest, but she barreled along. "It's nothing to be ashamed of, Harry. It happens to many of us. There's medications that might help. If it was me, I'd want you to tell me this. I'd want to have the best memory, the best mind possible for my loved ones. You've got such lovely grandchildren and amazing children. And Harry," she paused a minute, choking back the next words, "you have me, my darling. I love you with my whole heart. I want to spend as much time as possible with you as whole and healthy as we can."

Harry's eyes filled with tears. He pulled a hanky from his rumpled shirt pocket. "I'm sorry, Rose. I'm not the man you may have thought I was. I'm a shell of my former self. You deserve better."

"Nonsense. I fell in love with you at this age, Harry McMillen. It doesn't matter to me what you were like before. This is what I see before me now, a handsome man, a good heart, all of it, the total package. I'll say it again if you didn't hear me earlier. I love you. That's not easy for me to say."

When he didn't respond, she continued, "I want you to think about it. At least give some thought to what I've asked of you, okay? Would you do that for me?"

Harry nodded his head. Rising from the table, he shuffled over to Rose, pulling her up to him, burying his head in her shoulder, and years of grief poured from him.

"Rose, I have some things I'd like to get off my chest. Maybe once you've heard them, you'll feel differently about me. I do love you too, with my whole heart. But maybe, just maybe, you won't want me when you hear what I have to say."

Rose put a finger to Harry's lips. "Shhh," she said. "I don't want to know anything about your past. What's done is done for both of us. It's where we are right now that counts."

"I cheated on my wife, Rose. I was a pastor and I had an ongoing affair with our church secretary. Does that sound like the kind of man you want?"

Rose let go of Harry for a moment. Looking him fully in the face she said, "Well, I have my own sins too, mister. I got pregnant when I was seventeen. Back in the time when good girls didn't do that sort of thing. And guess what? I had an abortion. A back alley witchdoctor abortion. My parents forced me."

"I had no idea," Harry said. "Oh honey, oh Rose. . ." he kissed her then, her face, her neck; kissed her as if he could take all the bad away from them both.

"Please, Harry, just listen to me and listen to your children. Do what's right for your health. And let's both stop living in the past, okay?"

~*~

Later, when Harry had gone home, Rose lay in bed, an old

paperback propped on her chest, the glow of the light on her nightstand illuminating the book. Buttons curled next to her, purring while Rose reviewed the day. It had been scary, almost losing Harry, and then thinking he would come to hate her if she pressed the issue about his health. All in all it had gone well, and now Rose hoped he'd listen to her. The memory lapses were nothing to be ashamed of.

Rose fell asleep and dreamed of Skip that night. She dreamed that he and Harry's son Tim were talking in a funeral parlor while Rose watched from far away.

Chapter Sixteen

*T*he pounding on the front door woke Abby. She rolled over in bed and shook her husband's arm. "Tom, Tom, wake up. Someone's knocking. What on earth is the time?" Icy fear crystallized in Abby's stomach. She glanced at the clock. Seven a.m. It was Sunday. This couldn't be good.

Tom got out of bed, pulling a robe over his flimsy sweat pants. He parted the blinds, peering out the bedroom window that faced the front of the house. "It's Tim," he said.

Abby bolted out of bed. Just then Allison started fussing in her room. "Tom, please get the baby. I'll go down to my brother." Abby threw a sweatshirt and shorts on. Running down the stairs two at a time, she reached the front door, unlocking it. Her brother stood there, clean-shaven, hair in place. A crisp, white dress shirt and black pants. The best he'd looked in the longest time.

"Tim, what on earth?"

"Abby, I had to share this with you. I wanted you to see

me. Not just talk on the phone. Sorry about the hour." Tim brushed past her just as Tom headed down the stairs with the baby in his arms. Allison broke into smiles at the sight of her uncle, her little feet kicking.

"I'll make a pot of coffee," Abby said, then turning to her husband. "Are the boys up yet?"

"No, just the princess here."

Allison reached chubby hands toward her uncle. Tim pulled her into his arms, cradling her and laughing.

Abby looked over at Tom, who almost had a huge question mark appearing above his head.

As they walked into the kitchen, Tom spoke first. "So, Tim," he said, clearing his throat. "What, uh, brings you here at this hour?" Tom crossed his arms in front of himself, a slight smirk on his face.

Tim swung Allison around gently, crooning a soft song to her. "I'm sorry, I know it's awful early, but I had to share my news with you both. I'm going to be helping out at the new church in Greensburg. I got hired to help with their youth ministry."

Abby almost dropped the ceramic coffee mug she was holding. She stared at Tim as if he were a complete stranger. Yet in her heart, a warm glow began filling her. She'd always known there was good in her brother. Always known he had so much to offer.

"Sit down, here, have some coffee. Tell us all about it."

Tim told them after he'd met with Abby and gotten so much off his chest about the relationship with their father, he'd gone to Dad's old church and spoken with Pastor Freddy. He'd unloaded all the guilt he felt for his mother's death, all the shame he'd had over his father's behavior. Freddy, who'd known their family for many years, had listened to Tim and then prayed from his heart over him for clarity and direction. He'd asked Tim what he was most interested in. When Tim told him how strongly he felt for troubled young people, Freddy said he had a possible connection for him. The job at the new non-denominational church in Greensburg would be perfect for him.

"Also," Tim said, taking a sip of coffee while holding Allison against him, "I'm starting classes in the fall. I'm going to work with autistic children." The look on his face was beautiful. Abby couldn't describe it any other way. He almost glowed he was so happy.

"Oh Timmy," she said. "I can see why you wanted to share this with us. I'm so happy, so proud of you." Abby brushed a stray lock of hair from her face. Her throat constricted and she took a deep breath.

"Congratulations, Tim," Tom said clapping him on the back. "I've seen how good you are with Gavin. You'll do great with other autistic children."

An hour quickly passed and Tim rose from the table, handing Allison back to her father. "I've got to go. I don't want to be late for my first day. Wish me luck." He pecked Abby's cheek.

She walked him to the door and Tim turned to her. "I want to talk with Dad sometime. Pastor Freddy said I won't be totally free until I do this. It won't be easy. Pray for me, sis?"

Now Abby did start to cry. She held her brother tightly, not bothering to wipe the tears as they fell unbidden from her eyes, a torrent of pain she'd held back for so long.

"It's going to be alright, Timmy. It's going to be okay."

Tim McMillen couldn't believe how many people attended Greensburg Community Church. He'd grown up in the traditional old-fashioned setting, and here was a building that housed a café, children's nursery, youth wing, and huge sanctuary with a stage at the front. The music that played in the background sounded like rock, though he realized it was Christian in nature. Tim found himself liking this day very much.

He spoke to a group of young teens while their parents attended church. They met in a separate wing of the church, and here, at the podium, Tim looked out into the faces of youth and vigor and could see himself at that age, impressionable and eager. He had so much to tell them: His uphill battle with alcohol, his regrets, but mostly about his faith. He'd never lost it even though he'd been so bitter and angry for so many years. He still believed in God and prayed daily, hoping for a change, hoping God hadn't given up on him. He led them in prayer once he finished speaking, then their worship team played the amazing music.

Pastor Greg, the senior director of the church, asked Tim after services how he liked it. Tim couldn't talk fast enough, couldn't convey just how happy he was and how much it meant to him. He'd have other duties in the church, but for today, being in front of these young people, telling his story, he knew God had plans for him.

Chapter Seventeen

*D*r. Shoat shook his head. "Harry, I'm afraid medication won't be of much use to you. All the tests are confirmed. You do have dementia, but I'm confident yours is due to something fairly curable though."

Rose, Harry and Abby blew out their breath almost in unison. It was a relief hearing these words.

"From what your daughter described, and from the tests we've been running, I don't see a consistency of symptoms parallel with Alzheimer's. That, my friend is very good news." The doctor thumbed through a series of papers. "Here it is," he pointed to a paper about half way through the thick stack encased in a folder with Harry's name written on the front. "The blood work you had recently confirmed something for me. Your level of B-12 is dangerously low. B-12 is necessary for proper brain function. When the body becomes depleted, it can affect the part of the brain that helps us remember certain things. We can become confused, lose our way, so to speak."

Abby spoke first. "Dr. Shoat, what can be done for this?"

Dr. Shoat tapped his pen on the clipboard in front of him. "We can give your father B-12 injections, and he can take a daily supplement, but depending on how long he's had this problem he may never regain complete function. He may always become muddled or confused."

The doctor shuffled papers back into the folder.

"Doctor," Abby spoke up again. She had a notebook in front of her with questions lined up. The pen she gripped in her hand circled one of them over and over.

"I don't want to embarrass my father, but there is something that puzzles me most of all."

Dr. Shoat rose. "What is it?"

"My father seems to confuse my brother, Tim, for his brother Richard who passed away a few years ago." She looked at her father and saw Harry's face redden. "I'm sorry, Daddy, but I need to know about this. I think that's concerned me most of all lately: your confusion about Tim."

All eyes looked to Harry. He shifted in his seat uncomfortably. He tugged at the neckline of his Pittsburgh Pirates t-shirt.

The doctor put his hand on Harry's shoulder. "It's also not uncommon to hallucinate at times. I think the confusion, coupled with the fact that a person may remind them of someone perhaps. As long as it doesn't worsen, I think my friend Harry will do well." He patted Harry.

"Abby, I know my brother's gone," Harry said, a faraway look in his eyes. "It just hurts sometimes, seeing Tim and seeing my brother in him. I miss Richard so much. I guess to me, Tim is how I remember him most, vibrant and young. Even their mannerisms are similar."

The doctor turned to leave. As his hand touched the doorknob, he turned back with an afterthought.

"Now, young man, about using a cane. I think it's a wonderful idea. Marcy at the front desk will help you fill out some paperwork. I think we can get you fitted up with a right pretty model. Something befitting a good-looking devil like yourself." He winked at Rose.

"Thank you, Doc," Harry said. "It's a relief to hear this. I do get embarrassed when I mess something up. And there are times when it almost feels like my brain hurts when I try to think of something. But you're telling me these lapses will be few and far between. I guess the scariest was coming out of that bathroom and not knowing where I was headed."

"I understand, but I think with a good lady by your side, you won't have to worry about getting lost."

Rose felt herself flushing. Everyone seemed to think they'd been together for many years, though they'd only known one another for several months. Still, it was wonderful knowing Harry's progression wasn't devastating.

"Well, good luck, Harry," the doctor said. "Set up an appointment for a follow up with me in early November. We'll see how things turn out for you."

Abby walked ahead of her father and Rose and tapped the doctor on the back. "Were you just saying all that, or do you think my father is worse than he seems?"

"Your dad is a bright man. Maybe a bit stubborn, but a good sort. He'll have moments at times, and maybe he'll be a bit more unclear with certain situations. I've run all the tests though, and I'm not that worried, dear. You have a good day." The doctor disappeared into an office, closing the door.

On the drive back to Huntington, Harry sat in the back while Rose sat up front with Abby. Rose almost choked on the peppermint candy she'd taken from the receptionist's desk. Harry was talking softly and she'd heard a name.

"What did you just say, Harry?" Rose asked, as a creeping vine of fear edged itself into the pit of her belly.

"Oh, I'm just remembering Richard is all. I guess if I had him here, I'd give him a piece of my mind for leaving me so soon." Harry laughed.

"Harry," Rose turned in her seat to look directly at him. "Did your brother have a nickname, something you called him other than Richard?"

"Why, yes. Yes, he did. He went by the name Skip when we were young."

Now Rose did choke, but not on her candy. She felt her face pale. She felt her insides cramp. She felt a pang of regret so fierce it took the breath from her.

"What's the matter, Rose?" Abby asked.

Rose didn't hear her. "Harry," she said, without turning toward him this time. "Did your brother and you share the same last name?"

"No," Harry said. "He kept Angela's last name. Said he wanted a part of his mother with him always. It was tough on my parents adopting him legally and all. But the name stuck."

"Rose, you're scaring me," Abby said. Then recognition dawned on her face.

"Oh my gosh," Abby whispered. "The name, Rose, the name. You told me your story. You told me your beau's name was Skip." Abby gripped the steering wheel so hard, Rose was frightened for her.

"It's okay, Abby. A coincidence, maybe?" Rose didn't think so. This man, this wonderful man she'd fallen in love with in the golden years was Skip's brother? Could it be possible? If so, God certainly had a sense of humor.

They drove in silence the rest of the way. When they arrived back at Huntington, the day had turned a golden hue. The setting sun crested over the hill, the cicadas sang loudly in the branches of the trees.

"I want you both to come in for a bit, okay?" Rose asked.

"That is, if you have a little more time, Abby."

"Oh, I wouldn't miss this for the world." Abby climbed out of the mini-van, opening the doors for her father and Rose. When they entered Rose's apartment, Rose walked immediately over to her portrait on the wall.

"Harry, you told me you knew this picture, right?"

"Well, I thought I did," Harry said, scratching his head. "It reminded me of my brother's work. Now I'm not so sure."

"Come take a look at this signature," Rose pushed. "Tell me what you really see." She stood there with her heart hammering. Everything in her screamed it couldn't be possible. How could someone she knew and loved so many years ago come back to her this way? How could she possibly fall in love with his brother? It was all too much.

Harry pulled reading glasses from his light jacket pocket. Rose had turned the lights on in the living room. The scrawled, messy signature could have said anything. The large swirling "S," the capital "P" of the last name.

"Yes, my goodness," Harry said. He spoke the name out loud for the first time. "Skip Parkinson. My brother's painting." He looked at Rose, confusion on his face. "What, how?"

"Sit down, Harry. I have something to tell you." Abby and her father sat side by side as Rose settled into her rocker. The special chair she'd crocheted in so many nights. The chair she'd rocked her Thumbelina dolly in many days. Now it was to be a chair to tell a love story. A true love story.

As the night wore on, Rose watched Harry's face as he sat transfixed. She saw Abby brush at a tear several times. Yet she pressed on. Told the whole story as if her life depended on it. As she was about to finish, Harry interrupted her.

"Rose, my goodness. I haven't thought of that in years." His face held animation and shock. He looked at Rose as if he was seeing her for the first time. "It was me, Rose. I was the one who brought you the painting. I remember it now."

"That can't be possible," Rose said. The young man told me he was Skip's friend." Or had he? Rose couldn't remember clearly, but had Hunter ever said who he was?

"The man's name was Hunter who brought it," Rose said. "That couldn't have been you."

Harry laughed. Then he stood and walked over to Rose. Pulling her up by the hands and looking her in the face, the look on his face almost rapturous, he said, "I'm Hunter. That was what my brother called me."

Rose felt her knees buckling. It couldn't be. The end to this story, this unbelievable tale. Hunter, the man who'd held her when she was grieving. The man who'd told her just how much she meant to Skip. Here, before her. The man she now loved.

Abby, who had sat silently watching the drama unfolding,

jumped up from the couch and walked over to embrace her father and Rose. "Daddy, I never knew you and Uncle Richard had nicknames for each other." The three of them held one another, the sound of sniffling, the sound of laughter in the room.

"I don't believe it," Abby said. "This is so much more than a coincidence. How on earth?"

Harry turned from his girls, facing the portrait once again, his hand tracing the lines and swirls of the paintbrush strokes. "I guess Our Lord works in some very mysterious ways." He turned back to Rose.

"I don't remember too much, Rose, but a little is coming back to me now. I seem to remember thinking you were one of the prettiest gals I'd ever seen. Still do."

Abby shook her head, touching Rose, touching her father. "This is the most amazing love story I've ever heard."

Harry put his hands against Rose's face, cupping her gently with gnarled fingers. "I must have done something right in my life to be so blessed. I can't believe we found one another." He gazed into her eyes and Rose felt the years melting away, remembering how he'd looked as a teenager, remembering how kindly he'd treated her.

"I feel like I'm seventeen," Rose said. All of a sudden, Rose felt something break within her. The guilt she'd held onto all of her life, the blame, beginning to trickle away. Meeting

Harry was a gift, and it couldn't happen if she'd been a bad person, could it? Perhaps now, at this late age she could truly receive forgiveness.

Exhaustion overtook her, and Rose excused herself. Saying goodbye to Abby, then a long, warm embrace with Harry, she bid them both goodnight.

While she sat on the edge of her bed a little later, Rose whispered quietly to God. "I'm not sure what happened tonight, Lord, but I want to be free, truly free. I felt your presence and peace settling over me. I want you to know I'm trying to accept your gift of forgiveness. And God, thank you. Thank you for this miracle. Help me to make the best of my time with you at my side." Rose sighed. Getting up, she removed the vinyl baby doll, the one she'd called Nathaniel, from her chair, carefully wrapping it in tissue paper from her dresser drawer, and placing it into a box in the far corner of her closet. Nothing stirred in her; after all, it was only a memento, something she'd used at the most difficult times of her life. She wouldn't need it any longer.

Chapter Eighteen

*T*oni sat at the outside café on Grant Street in downtown Pittsburgh nibbling at her salad, but mostly pushing food around on her plate. She'd lost her appetite and secretly wished for an early drink. The lunch crowd thinned a bit, and she and Ben were the only two left on the patio.

The dinner with her mother had unnerved her. Toni still couldn't believe how different, how normal Mother seemed. The gentleman friend, Harry, was a delight. Toni could see how much they cared for one another.

Ben sat across from her, making small talk, his suit jacket casually laid over the back of the wrought iron chair, doing his best to distract her.

"You haven't heard a word I said, did you?" he asked, rubbing his thumb over her hand. "I give up. What's on your mind, Toni?"

Toni signaled the waitress. "I'll have a vodka and tonic, please."

"Whoa, a little early in the day, missy," Ben said, waggling his finger at her. "Toni's being a bad little girl."

"Nobody will smell the vodka on my breath at the office. I'm fine."

"Well, I'm not going to join you. I'm not giving them a chance to find any dirt on me." Ben stopped rubbing her hand and sat back in his chair, his direct gaze unnerving.

"I guess I've had it all wrong," Toni said as the waitress set the drink before her. "I've lived a lie, I think, and I've done my best to alienate the woman who loves me more than anything else. I've played hardball so much in my professional life, and thought it would get me through in my personal life as well."

"I see it as a gift," Ben said. "You've been given a chance to see your mother in a whole new light. Not many people who've been estranged from loved ones are so lucky."

The vulnerable little girl in Toni screamed to be set free. "I don't know anything about my mother," Toni said, sipping her drink. "Why she and Grandmother never got along. I always thought it was my mom's weakness and mental issues. There may be things I don't even realize."

Toni paused. Her mind fluttered to the times Gram Ruth and Mama had been around one another in the later years. It was as if two poisonous snakes slow-danced around each other, waiting for the other to trip, to make just one bad move.

Why did Gram always treat Mama so unkindly? Was that what rubbed off on Toni and did she feel absolved for harboring such ill feelings toward her mother because of her grandmother's actions?

"Ben, I can't help but think there's some missing piece in all this. Something I don't know about my mother. If I'd only given her a chance earlier. Do you think it's too late for us now?"

"Toni, she glowed when she was with you. Did you see her smiling? I don't think it's ever too late." Ben ran his fingers through his hair. "You gave me a second chance, right?" He winked at her.

Exasperated, Toni couldn't help but smile at him. He'd hurt her so terribly, yet he'd helped her crack her tough exterior to find the little girl inside herself who had a tender heart after all. Life was strange and unpredictable.

"I'm going to call her tonight," Toni said, fishing her car keys from her leather bag. "I'm going to set up another time to get together with her. Maybe, just maybe, I'll find some answers." She got up and pecked Ben briefly on the cheek.

"Hey, is that all I get?" he asked.

"You've got to earn my affection, *honey.*" She emphasized the word, wiggled her fingers at him and was gone.

Chapter Nineteen

Crystal Gates pulled her long, knee length boots up her slender legs. She sat on the edge of the bed, her blonde spiky hair sticking up in every direction. Tim saw the look she gave him, a look of question and almost disgust.

"Who're you trying to be today?" she asked him. "My father?" She dragged on her Virginia Slims cigarette, crushing it in the ashtray on the night stand.

"I wish you wouldn't smoke in here," Tim said, unbuttoning his shirt. "You know I can't stand it."

"What's with the Halloween costume?" Crystal asked, zipping the second boot.

"I got a job. I tried telling you the other night, but you were too out of it," Tim said.

"You're accusing me? I seem to remember you being out of it yourself." Crystal stood, glaring at Tim now, her long fingernail pointing at his chest.

"Sorry, babe," Tim said. "It's just, well, I wanted to try to make some changes is all. I, uh, I got a small job at a church."

Crystal laughed then. Not a happy sound at all. A mocking, almost taunting sound in the stillness of the room they shared.

"Church?" she snickered. "You gonna be a pastor like your daddy?"

"Stop it, would you," Tim snapped. "I'm trying to be serious. I'm going to work with their youth program. I'm no pastor. . ." Tim trailed off.

"Well, holy boy," Crystal jeered, "how about driving me to work tonight and staying on a little?" She sidled up to him, trying to be cute and coy. "Please," she pouted.

Tim struggled with this. Part of him screamed, stay as far away from her nightclub as you can. Yet there was that other side to him that said, just one drink, that's all. One won't hurt, much, anyway.

He gathered her into his arms, his chin resting on her head, the gel tickling him from her hair. "Okay, I'll take you, babe. I'll just stay a little while though, okay?"

~*~

Later that night, Tim would eat his words. There was no such thing as staying a short time, or having one drink. The minute he headed into the old atmosphere of a smoke-filled lounge, pool tables and juke boxes, it was all over. There wasn't a coherent thought in his head about what he'd done earlier. It was as if Crystal and the life he led with her could erase everything else. Thoughts of trying to talk with his father faded, replaced with the old feelings of anger in the pit of his stomach. What was he thinking earlier today? How weak-willed was he after all? It was his dad who needed to apologize. His dad who needed to make amends for a lifetime of pain. No, as Tim downed one more Coors, and Crystal poured him a shot of whiskey as a chaser, the numb feeling soothed him and more than ever, Tim knew he'd come home.

The next day, Tim rolled over in bed, his tongue sticking to the roof of his cottony mouth. His head screamed in pain and he covered his eyes from the brightness of the morning sun pouring through the only window in the room. *What have I done?* He remembered bringing Crystal to work, remembered having a few drinks. *A few?* Remembered slow dancing with Crystal at some point, but nothing beyond that.

How did we get home? This thought, above all else frightened Tim. The fact he remembered nothing about driving, whether it was he or Crystal, neither of them should have driven.

She lay on her side, her face still caked with makeup, lips parted slightly, snoring. A wave of disgust washed over Tim, followed quickly by his old friend: guilt. Was he disgusted with her? Or was it himself? How about both of them? Yes, that sounded more like it. Tim threw everything away in one night. All that he'd built up the day before. The story he shared with the youth at church, the fact he believed so strongly in God, just chucked it right out the window.

God, I'm so sorry. Tim felt nothing. No still, small voice, no absolution.

I'm a weak man. Yes, that was the truth. Now he felt like he was getting somewhere. Admitting it was good, wasn't it?

And the last thought: *I can't do this anymore.* What was it that he couldn't do? Continue working at a church, or partying? Why couldn't he have both? Yet he knew in his heart it wouldn't be possible.

Crystal opened one bloodshot eye. "Hey, good-looking," she mumbled.

Tim put a shaky hand out intending to gently stroke her cheek. Instead, he pulled it back, everything inside him screaming to leave now. Leave, and never return.

"I'm going to make some coffee," he announced, and got up to retrieve discarded clothing that littered the floor.

Around noon, Tim headed outside with his cell phone. He'd misbuttoned his shirt, but didn't care. He kept looking around, almost afraid Crystal would see him and start asking questions. He dialed a number.

The phone rang several times before going to voice mail.

"Hey, you've reached Fred Andrews. Leave a message, please."

Tim debated a moment. Pastor Fred would check his messages later in the day. He always did. Tim needed him now though. He climbed the rickety staircase that led into the apartment above the dental office, his home for the last eight months, and called through the screen door.

"Crys, I'll be back. I have an errand to run." Tim didn't wait to hear her voice. He knew he needed to split before she asked too many questions.

He drove around Latrobe for an hour. Tim couldn't bring himself to enter the old church. The dark gray stone façade stood sentinel, beckoning. Yet many thoughts roiled within. Good thoughts of his family back in the day long before his father's indiscretion. Thoughts of himself and his siblings,their closeness and happy times. On the tail end of these thoughts, however, was the very last time he'd attended this church: The funeral of his mother. Harry had been retired by then, too old to officiate at his own wife's service. But the rift had begun that day, Tim and Harry barely speaking to one another. After the procession to the cemetery, Tim knew he'd his father was lost to him.

He tried telling himself through the years it would pass. One day, he and Dad would hug one another, clap each other on the back and have a good laugh together. That never happened. Once Tim saw his father's mental decline, he attributed the moodiness when they were around each other to the fact that his father probably had old-timers disease. He never thought Harry would carry a grudge so long. That the time he'd slapped his son in the face, accusing him of killing his mother, would end any hope of ever getting along again.

Chapter Twenty

*R*ose awoke, the happiest she'd been in a long time. It was true. Harry and Skip were brothers and she'd known Harry in her youth. He'd been the kind young man who'd brought her the painting of herself. The one her darling had painted from memory. It was unreal, but Rose felt giddy and light. She couldn't wait to see Harry today.

As she made her bed, Rose thought about Toni. It had been wonderful seeing her daughter, spending quality time with her and the young man. Rose wondered if she and Toni would ever grow close enough to have a more serious talk. Perhaps Rose needed to come clean about what happened in her past, especially since the past had come back in such a major way.

When the timing was right, Rose thought she might be able to do it. The talk was such a long time coming.

~*~

A soft knock on her door brought Rose from the kitchen. She just finished drying a few coffee cups and still had the dishtowel in her hands.

Harry stood on the porch with his silver hair neatly combed and wearing a pale blue shirt that accentuated his eyes. For a moment he seemed a young man. He reached out his hand to stroke her cheek. Rose dropped the cloth she'd been holding as they fell into each other's arms.

"I could barely sleep," Harry said, nuzzling into her neck. "I still can't believe this, Rose. How can it be?"

A car drove by, its horn tooting as the two lovers stood embracing. A man and woman waved to them, huge smiles on their faces.

"Come on in, Harry. We'll be arrested for a public display of affection or something."

"I want to talk with you about that day, Rose. I want to see what we both remember."

Seated on the couch, fingers interlaced as they held hands, Rose took a deep breath. She glanced over at the portrait of herself. Almost willing herself back to the day, back in time.

The week before Rose would begin the private all-girls school, she'd been sketching a charcoal drawing at the side porch of her house. It felt wonderful being outside again, away from the prison of her bedroom. Rose had chosen a bouquet of daisies her father gave her a few days before. They sat in a milk glass vase upon the table top in front of her. Rose had her feet propped up, the sketch pad on her lap when she heard a car door. Looking up from her work, she saw a teenage boy, maybe eighteen or nineteen walking across her lawn. Rose had never seen him before. Rather tall and a bit too thin, perhaps, he was handsome in an almost military manner: Very straight back and crew cut. Yet the most outstanding feature of the boy was his eyes. Piercing blue eyes, she could spot even at the distance she sat from him, made her heart catch in her throat? Who was he?

The boy cleared his throat, and he seemed a bit nervous at first as he approached. Rose put down her charcoal pencil and lay her sketch pad upon the table. She stood and called out to him.

"May I help you?"

"I'm looking for Rose. Rose Whittaker. I have a delivery for her." Again, he cleared his throat, and now he stood before her, visibly shaken.

Rose glanced out across the expanse of her lawn at the beat-up old car parked in front of her house. There was no delivery truck. Fear shot through her belly and she turned to call out to her brother. She found herself looking back at the young man, though. Not usually curious by nature, and most certainly not unusually brave, Rose spoke up. "Who are you? What business do you have?"

The young man stared at Rose and it felt like he was staring into her soul. Those eyes. . .

"Are you, uh, Rose?" he asked.

"I don't see a delivery truck," Rose said, crossing her arms before her. Yet the fear she'd felt moments before vanished as the young man's face broke into a smile.

"Skip said you were a pistol."

At the name of her beloved, Rose relaxed. "Skip?"

"I'm sorry. Allow me to introduce myself. The name's Hunter."
The young man bowed before Rose, took her hand and kissed it delicately.
Rose broke into a fit of giggles.

"Oh, brother," she said. "This better be good."

"Well you see, Skip has a gift for you. Something he wanted to
bring you himself, but I guess your father wouldn't allow him to see you.
Am I right?"

Rose liked Hunter. For his age he was witty and charming, a
regular ladies' man.

"Yes," Rose whispered. "I'm never to see him again."

Still holding onto her hand, Hunter led her across the yard to his
vehicle. Rose stole glances back at her house every so often. If Mother was
watching, she'd be in huge trouble.

Hunter opened the door to his Dodge, and Rose saw the large brown
paper parcel she'd seen under Skip's arms several weeks ago.

"Now, before I give this to you, Skip wanted me to tell you a few
things, okay?" Hunter leaned against the side of his car. He pulled a note
from his pocket and read aloud:

"My dearest Rose. I am not allowed to see you. I tried to bring you
this gift a few weeks ago, but your father would not let me. I could not get
you off my mind, so I tried to capture in this portrait your innocence, your
goodness and your beauty. Please accept this small token of my love for you
and know it was good and true. I would have done anything for you my
darling Rose. I would have gone to the ends of the earth for you and I

certainly would have married you to raise our child together. My heart aches for you and my body longs for you. I will never forget you and pray you never forget me. May you always remember the love I carried for you when you view this painting. If there was something, anything I could do to be reunited with you, I hope to learn of it. Until then, I remain always yours, Skip."

Rose took the note from Hunter, hugging it to her chest, the smell of it, Skip's cologne, still clinging to it.

Hunter held the package while Rose slipped the note into her blouse pocket. She saw him watching her as she ripped the brown paper. Her eyes widened when she saw the stunning likeness of herself. She stifled a small cry as Hunter continued holding the canvas. The painting was exquisite, a perfect likeness of Rose sitting on her porch. When she pictured the time involved to paint such a glorious picture, she knew in her heart just how much she'd been loved by Skip. A love like theirs would stand the test of time, and if it was possible, one day they would find one another again.

Harry sat motionless as Rose told her side of the story. He stole a look at the painting before he spoke.

"Rose, you did find him again. In me. Your wish, your prayer came true, don't you see? What a blessing this is, what a perfect ending to the love you two had between you."

Harry pulled Rose up and they strolled over to the portrait. "He talked of little else after I brought it to you. I remember that now. For weeks, I watched my brother pining away.

"One night he had a little too much to drink, and he'd told me he drove past your home around three in the morning. It took everything in him not to walk up to the door and insist to see you. Sometimes, I don't think he was ever the same."

Harry put his arms around Rose. The embrace, a gift from his brother, so long gone.

"Harry, do you mind telling me what happened to him?"

"Skip and I both went into the service, but he saw a little more action than I did. He was wounded by flying shrapnel and sent home with an honorable discharge and received a medal of honor. He never walked right after that, though, because the pieces had embedded themselves deeply into his knee.

"He took on a job as some of us did at local steel mills back in their heyday, and he never married. Oh, he had a few ladies through the years, but I remember one time, oh, maybe a year or two before he died, he mentioned your name again.

"He said to me, 'Hunter, I had a good one, Rosie. I don't think you get a chance like that again.' He passed away from liver failure in his early sixties. Drink got to him, you see. It was his most powerful weakness."

"I can't believe he never married," Rose said. "Did he ever paint again?"

"Yes, that was the one thing he loved. He never sold any portraits, only did them for people who asked. I think he felt it was his atonement."

"Oh Harry," Rose shook her head. "I lived my whole life needing atonement. I guess we both had our regrets."

"Rose, he mentioned the baby to me. Said he would have loved to be a daddy."

"Harry, do you think God will forgive me?"

"Rose, honey, you didn't mean for any of it to happen. Why have you always felt such a burden of guilt?"

"I guess it was because of Mother," Rose said. "She shipped me off to that all-girls school so that I wouldn't ever disgrace the family again. She told me God would never forgive me for bringing a life into the world, a life that had to end because it was so wrong."

"That's horrible," Harry said. "No wonder you had such a time of it where church was concerned. I imagine that's always why you felt such shame."

"I was hospitalized through my twenties and early thirties. I had a nervous breakdown, Harry. All that burden. I couldn't bear it."

"My poor Rose," Harry said, leading her away from the painting. "Let's attend church together this weekend. Perhaps you'll begin to find the true healing you've been searching for. What do you think?"

Rose fidgeted with the buttons on her blouse, unable to meet Harry's eye. After a moment she said, "Yes, I'll go with you."

Chapter Twenty-One

On one of the first crisp fall days, Tim McMillen slipped into the back row of Trinity Episcopal. He couldn't bring himself to go back this weekend to Greensburg Community Church. He'd lied to Pastor Greg, lied to protect himself. He couldn't face the young people again after messing up so badly. No, he needed some quiet time in an old, familiar setting to do a bit of reflecting. Leaning against the pew in front of him, Tim clasped his hands together and shut his eyes.

~*~

Harry and Rose entered the old church, the one he'd pastored for many years. The smell of Murphy's oil soap and candlewax brought a nostalgic feeling to Rose. As a little girl, her father had taken her to a church like this. That was one memory she didn't associate with guilt. She and her brother enjoyed the weekly services as children. The songs were the best part. Mother had never gone with them, and Rose wondered about that through the years. She'd preached and railed like a doomsday prophet, but never had anyone seen the woman step foot in any church.

Rose clutched Harry's arm, walking with him through the foyer. "Harry," she whispered, "I don't want to sit up real close. Perhaps somewhere in the back, okay?"

Harry guided her to one of the back pews. A young man was the only other person in the row. His head was down, and he looked up as they slid into their seat.

Recognition dawned on Rose's face as she gazed into the hazel eyes of Tim McMillen. He had dark circles under his eyes and the beginnings of a beard on his face. His longer hair was combed away from his face, and at this close range, Rose could only think of Skip.

Tim's eyes widened when he realized who was sitting next to him. He turned to exit the other side of the pew, but a family of four had already sat down. Feeling like a cornered criminal, he smiled shyly at Rose, then opened a prayer book pretending to study the readings.

Rose didn't mention to Harry the fact that his estranged son sat next to her. She knew he hadn't seen him yet and perhaps that was good. The service began and everyone in the congregation stood.

Throughout her time in church, Rose felt better than she

had in years. It wasn't scary after all, and she believed the words the pastor spoke of on healing and forgiveness.

Out of the corner of her eye, Rose noticed how nervous Tim appeared. He bounced his left leg up and down, drumming his fingers against his dress slacks. And as the service approached its close, Rose couldn't figure out what to do.

Do I tell Harry? Do I leave this alone? He's always telling me about letting go. Maybe this is his time.

The last song was sung and Harry turned to exit the pew. Rose tugged on his sleeve and whispered in his ear. "I think there's someone you need to see."

Harry had a puzzled expression on his face, but as Rose shifted slightly, his eyes widened at the sight of his son.

People were leaving now, talking and shaking hands. Harry, Rose and Tim stood waiting as the church cleared.

When silence had descended, Rose excused herself. "I need to find the ladies room," she said. "I'll hold up the senior van, Harry. Take your time." She patted Tim's arm as he gave her a pleading look.

~*~

God, I didn't think you'd throw me into a situation like this. Tim looked down as Rose left the pew. Harry glared at his son.

"H-hello Dad," he said. Nothing.

Tim tried to touch his father's sleeve, but the man pulled

away from him, his lower lip pouting, his jaw clenched in anger.

"What do you want from me?" Tim asked. "How long is this rift between us going to go on? I can't sleep, I can't eat, I can't hold down a job. Are you happy, old man?"

"There's nothing to say," Harry said. "You hate me and you hurt your mother to prove just how much." He turned to go.

Tim grabbed his father's sleeve. "Listen to me, will you? I came here today to try and figure out how I could make things up to you. How I could change. You gotta believe me, Dad. I want this over with."

Tim sat down hard into the wooden pew. He raked his hands through his hair. Harry stood above him, lip quivering.

"All the years I pastored here, I preached similar sermons to the one we heard today. Forgiveness, and letting go of spite. Never in my wildest dreams did I ever think my own son would betray me. Never did I think he'd have such hatred and ill feelings to the point of hurting the gentlest creature in the world, his mother. How can I let that go?

"I'm a weak man, Skip. I'm not sure I ever had what it takes to be a godly man."

Tim looked up when his father called him Skip. He shook his head. Nothing would change. He had to move on. He had to come to grips with the fact his father was never going to forgive him. He was as good as dead to him.

~*~

When Rose slipped back into the church, she saw Tim slide out the other end of the pew and exit quickly.

"Harry, what happened? Were you two able to talk?"

Harry shook his head and grabbed Rose's hand. "Let's go."

Chapter Twenty-Two

Rose bustled around her apartment, rearranging pillows on the couch. Toni was due in a few minutes for her first crocheting lesson. Rose never dreamed this day would come: A day when they could truly be mother and daughter enjoying one another's company. All the feelings she'd held bottled up for so long, now flowed unbidden. The feeling of always having to keep herself in check, of pretending everything was normal, when Rose had no control of the situation.

A knock sounded at her door, and Rose let her daughter in. Toni embraced her mother, perhaps a bit more tightly than she ever had.

"Mama," she said, "thank you for seeing me today. I'm excited to learn from you."

While they were seated on the sofa a little later, Toni began to ask questions. They came pouring from her from somewhere deep inside, a floodgate breached, a dam opened.

Rose could hardly contain herself for the years' worth of questions her daughter asked. She had to be careful not to paint Grandma Ruth in a bad light. Though the woman was the cause of most of Rose's own heartache, perhaps she, too, had reasons for being the hardened creature she'd been.

"I'm parched," Rose said. "All this talking has made my tongue stick to the roof of my mouth. Let's get some lemonade, shall we?" The two headed into the kitchen.

While Rose poured from the pitcher, Toni barreled straight ahead.

"Mama, I guess I need to know something else. We've spoken of so many things today, but we skirted around your hospital stays. Can you tell me? Will you tell me?"

Rose took a deep breath and after a long drink of lemonade, she crossed her arms in front of her. "You deserve it, Toni. You need to hear it all, not just the fluff. I didn't want to taint your view of your grandmother, but I have to give it to you straight."

"Mama, no matter how much it hurts either you or me, I need to hear this. I promise I won't think less of you. I've told you before, I'm sorry for the pictures I painted of you in my own mind. I realize there are reasons people go through what they do. I need to know."

The look on her daughter's face, the pleading, almost innocent look of a child decided Rose. She told Toni everything then. All about Skip, the pregnancy, the abortion, all of it. When she was finished, her daughter wiped her eyes with a paper napkin. This time the look on Toni's face was much different. Through all the years of raising this girl, disgust, shame, haughtiness had all been the palette which made up her daughter's countenance. Now Rose saw only one thing. Love.

Toni rose from the table, embracing her mother. Years of grief poured from her. Grief for what they'd lost in their early years, grief for not knowing the whole story. A flood of healing took its place and for the first time Toni really meant it when she said, "I love you, Mama."

Chapter Twenty-Three

*T*im McMillen sat in front of Westmoreland Community College. He hadn't slept well the night before, and this morning he was due to begin taking classes. When he was younger, he'd gotten his liberal arts degree. Now he was headed back to begin the early childhood development classes which would permit him to work with special needs children.

What his sister Abby didn't know, nor possibly even their father, was Tim's other secret. Only his mother had known and carefully guarded it from her husband and family.

Tim mulled over the reasons he'd agreed to taking classes so much later in life. He loved his nephew Gavin who'd so recently been diagnosed with a mild form of autism. He wanted to be helpful to his sister and brother-in-law to share with them what he'd learn. More than that, he wanted to finally come to grips with his own diagnosis so long ago. The shame he'd felt when Mom took him to Dr. Perry's office when he was around ten years old and learned he had a form of autism.

Not only that, but a strange variation where Tim blurted out hurtful phrases and sentences. Tim had taken medication most of his life and no one knew. Nobody realized the reasons he couldn't hold down jobs, couldn't socialize like they all did. Why he chose some of the relationships with women that he did. Nobody knew that years of alcohol abuse was a form of escape from the fears he held inside, the social anxiety that plagued him daily.

Tim almost told his sister this past summer, almost spilled the whole truth. The fact she wondered why nobody in her family or Tom's ever had autism had puzzled her when her little boy had gotten the diagnosis.Tim's blanketing guilt over holding this information from his sister added to the guilt he felt over Mom's death.

My father will never forgive me. This thought, more than any other cut deep inside. Tim opened the door to his truck and vomited. Looking around, he quickly wiped his mouth with the back of his hand, smoothed his hair and took a deep breath.

Abby's cell phone rang. She saw Rose's name in the window. Allison who'd been asleep on her lap stirred as her mother shifted her.

"Hi Rose, how are you?"

"I have to talk to you about something," Rose said.

For the next twenty minutes, Rose poured out from her

heart what she'd been holding back since she met Harry. She told Abby about the fight he had with Tim the day Harry moved in. She told the girl about the church incident, and how hard and unforgiving Harry had seemed. It puzzled her. A man, especially a pastor, who so easily preached forgiving others, harbored the most ill-feelings toward his own son, especially a son who was so willing to ask his father to let go of his anger.

Abby blew out a long breath. Allison slept on, while Abby's inner turmoil raged. That she loved and forgave her father for all he'd done in the past was a certainty. And now what she knew about Timmy, how he'd purposely hurt their dad to get back at him, well, she loved her brother. She would have to let this go too. What could she do?

Tim shifted from one foot to the other. His shirt clung to his back, sweat pouring between his shoulder blades in the stickiness of the unusually humid autumn day. Abby stood next to him, determination on her face. She knocked again at their father's apartment door, and then grabbed her brother's hand.

"I don't think this will work," Tim said, trying to swallow, but his tongue stuck to the roof of his mouth. "What makes you think it'll be so different?"

Abby didn't answer, just knocked again, knowing Rose

was inside with her father, and buying a little time.

The door opened a crack, and Rose peered out, a knowing smile breaking out onto her face.

"Come in, you two," she said.

The smell of fresh-baked bread permeated the apartment. Tim walked in but saw no sign of his father.

"Did you tell him?" Rose asked Abby. When the girl shook her head, Rose smiled again, a secret passing between the two women. Rose took hold of Tim's arm and led him into the kitchen.

"Harry, Skip is here to see you," she said.

Harry who had been slicing into the fresh, crusty loaf of bread at the counter, turned. His eyes met Tim's and a huge smile lit up his face.

Rose continued holding onto Tim. Abby stayed behind in the living room.

Tim had no idea what was going on, but as his heart pounded in his chest, he began to see more clearly.

Harry put the bread aside, wiping his hands on the dish towel. He walked over to his son and was about to embrace him when his face clouded, and a scowl immediately replaced the beaming smile which had just been there.

"That's no way to greet your brother, is it?" Rose asked.

Harry scratched his head. Tim could see the puzzlement within.

"Now, Hunter," Rose said, "Give Skip a hug. After all, how long has it been?"

"You're not Skip," Harry said. "You're Tim." His voice held the first tenderness in a long time when he said his son's name. "My brother's gone." Harry stared off into the distance. "My goodness, you look so like him," he said to no one in particular. "He was my best friend, not just a half-brother. He was so self-destructive. I don't think he ever got over that girl from when he was younger."

Tim stood still, the scene before him unnerving. If he could bolt from the room, he would. But Rose held onto him.

Harry broke from his reverie and looked from Rose to Tim. "What is this?"

"Harry, I wanted you to see Tim for who he really is. I know sometimes you get confused. I know you look at him and think you see your brother. But the man standing here before you is a good man, your son. And he loves you with his whole heart. He wants to tell you just how much. And Harry, he wants your forgiveness."

Abby walked into the room then. Standing next to her brother and Rose, she nudged Tim's shoulder. "Tell him," she said.

With the two women on either side of him, Tim took a deep breath.

"Dad, I'm so sorry about hurting you. I'm sorry I upset

you and Mom. I don't know what else I can do to make it up to you. I want you to try and understand something." Tim closed his eyes and shuddered. It was now or never.

"You need to know about me," he said, opening his eyes and staring into his father's face. "I sometimes can't control what I say. When I blurted out what happened to Mom, I wasn't trying to hurt you or her, honest. I have a condition, a problem. It's a disorder. I sometimes say things I shouldn't. Sometimes my tongue works faster than my brain, and bad things come out, sometimes swear words, sometimes hurtful phrases.

"It was something Mom knew about, but she never wanted anyone in the family to find out. She knew how much it embarrassed me when I was little. It's called Asperger's. You see, I have something similar to Abby's son, Gavin. I have a form of autism that has affected me all my life, especially socially.

"I admit, I was angry with you for some of the things you did, but I never intended for Mom to have that stroke. I wasn't taking my medication at that time, and my symptoms were really bad. I know that sounds like a poor excuse, but from what I've been reading and learning, it's the truth."

Harry looked down at the floor. "I- I still don't understand."

"Daddy," Abby said, "sometimes we don't completely

understand what happens in life. It's like you and Rose. I think we're given chapters of life, certain moments to go through, and when one chapter closes, another opens. You loved Mom with your whole heart, and now you have another woman who adores you. You are truly blessed, and it's time to move on and make new memories, time to move past old hurts and regrets. In time, we'll explain Tim's condition to you a little better. But for now, it's enough to know he never meant to hurt you or Mom. Can you find it in your heart to let go and forgive him?"

Chapter Twenty-Four

*R*ose stood looking out the window. Toni put the finishing touches to her mother's hair and makeup.

"You look absolutely stunning, Mama. It's no wonder you found love again."

Rose turned and smiled at her daughter. "This is one of the happiest days of my life." She reached out to touch her daughter's face. "You're certainly part of the reason." Rose sighed and picked up the small bouquet of white roses which lay on the table of the sitting room of the Thistledown at Seger House Inn.

"You don't think I'm foolish?" Rose asked, placing the flowers under her nose and taking a deep breath of the scent.

"No, Mama." Toni smiled as Ben entered the room.

"Whoa, who's the beautiful lady?" He kissed Rose on the cheek. She put her hand up to touch the place where his lips grazed her face.

"Love is a strange thing," Rose said, turning back to look out the window. "You never think you'll find it again, and sometimes when you do, it's in the most unlikely of places."

Abby entered the room. "Rose, are you almost ready?"

"Yes, dear. I was just saying how odd love is. When you're a teenager, you think you've found love. Your world caves in when it doesn't work out. Eventually, you marry and raise a family. Love of your children takes over then, and you sometimes lose a little of the reason you cared for your husband in the first place.

"I never dreamed I'd find love in the golden years. Never thought such a complete circle of love would return to me. Mature love takes the place of silly school girl crushes. You both know so much about the world because you've lived your lives already. You see things for what they really are. No, he's not the dashing hero he may have once been. Health issues and memory problems, bent bodies and even the thought of losing one another are all too certain. But you love despite all that. When it's good and true, nothing, not even old age can take that away from you."

"Come, Mama, they're ready." Toni kissed her mother's cheek as Tim walked into the room. He reached for Rose's hand and guided her out the door.

~*~

Rose descended the lush, carpeted staircase, her eyes lighting upon the enormous stained-glass window in front of her. She smiled thinking about the night before. Rose, Toni and Abby had stayed in one of the rooms of the charming, renovated inn, giggling like schoolgirls late into the night. They'd enjoyed the lavish accommodations and sumptuous meal the innkeeper, Michelle, had so thoughtfully made them.

As Rose continued down the stairs, holding onto Tim's arm, she waved to Michelle who stood beaming a beautiful smile at her.

"I wish you all the best, Rose," she said and opened the double doors to the front porch. Rose couldn't believe her eyes. On the street was a horse-drawn carriage, the stately driver tipped his hat to her as she and Tim approached. Tim helped her inside and they sat together with Abby and Toni as the horses pulled them ahead.

Peace settled within her as Rose was drawn the two blocks to the Ligonier town diamond and gazebo. She thought about the wedding she'd witnessed several months before, never dreaming she'd be the guest of honor on such a day.

Guitar music began playing and all the people seated rose to their feet.

Abby and her children walked first, the rust-colored dress setting off Abby's auburn hair. Gavin and Nicholas stood on either side of their mother in khaki pants and matching polo shirts. Allison in a long pink dress with lacy ribbons toddled in front of them at her father's prompting, a small basket of flowers clutched in chubby hands.

Harry came next from the back of the crowd, escorted by

Rose's daughter Toni. He leaned upon a shiny, black cane for support. As always, his air of dignity gave him the look of authority, but something had changed. His eyes were clear and his features softened. Anyone who'd known him before would swear they saw something very different in him.

Finally, all eyes focused on the image of Rose as she walked onto the lawn holding onto Tim's arm. The lacy chiffon dress and the new hairstyle made her look at least 10 years younger. She nodded at several people from Huntington, nurses and a few friends.

Tim held his arm at his side with Rose's delicate hand clasped tenderly beneath. Never before had he felt so proud or so happy to be a part of something. Tim's fears were gone for this day, replaced only by love.

As Rose and Tim strode forward to where Harry stood under the gazebo with Pastor Fred, Tim's eyes met his father's for a moment. A huge smile broke out onto Harry's face and as Tim brought Rose to his dad, Harry stopped. He reached out to his son, embracing him, and said the words Tim thought he'd never hear. "I love you, Son."

Rose and Harry recited their marriage vows on an autumn day, beneath a blue sky dotted with wispy clouds. A slight wind picked up with the promise of a winter chill yet to come, but for this day they rejoiced in the warmth of a love woven in time.

About the Author

Karen Malena lives in Western, Pennsylvania. Her compassion toward others is evident in her writings and blogs. Her interests include reading, weekend trips with her husband, music and nature. Karen is active in her town encouraging others to write through local library programs and author events. She's a member of Pittsburgh East Scribes, a monthly writing group.

Other books by Karen Malena

Reflections from my Mother's Kitchen (Lamb Books)
Shadow of my Father's Secret
Piggy

Karen Malena